The Ghost
in the Mirror

BOOKS BY JOHN BELLAIRS

The Ghost in the Mirror

The Mansion in the Mist

The Secret of the Underground Room

The Chessmen of Doom

The Trolley to Yesterday

The Lamp from the Warlock's Tomb

The Eyes of the Killer Robot

The Revenge of the Wizard's Ghost

The Spell of the Sorcerer's Skull

The Dark Secret of Weatherend

The Mummy, the Will, and the Crypt

The Curse of the Blue Figurine

The Treasure of Alpheus Winterborn

The Letter, the Witch, and the Ring

The Figure in the Shadows

The House with a Clock in Its Walls

THE GHOST IN THE MIRROR

JOHN BELLAIRS
Completed by Brad Strickland

Frontispiece
by Edward Gorey

Dial Books for Young Readers
New York

Published by
Dial Books for Young Readers
A Division of Penguin Books USA Inc.
375 Hudson Street
New York, New York 10014

Printed in the U.S.A.
First Edition
1 3 5 7 9 10 8 6 4 2

Library of Congress Cataloging in Publication Data
Bellairs, John.
The ghost in the mirror / John Bellairs ;
completed by Brad Strickland.—1st ed.
p. cm.
Summary: Rose Rita Pottinger and Mrs. Zimmermann are
transported back to 1828 to save the Weiss family from
being destroyed by a wicked wizard.
ISBN 0-8037-1370-3 : —ISBN 0-8037-1371-1 (lib.) :
[1. Time travel—Fiction. 2. Supernatural—Fiction.]
I. Strickland, Brad. II. Title.
PZ7.B413Gh 1993 [Fic]—dc20 92-18369 CIP AC

The Ghost
in the Mirror

CHAPTER ONE

For seven nights in a row Mrs. Zimmermann had seen weird things in her front parlor. Each night, around twelve, she would wake up and go downstairs to watch the strange lights that played on her walls and ceiling. Sometimes she saw eerie pictures on the blank wall in the passageway outside the pantry. Once she saw a sad little girl who seemed to be beckoning to her. Other times she saw smiling faces and a graveyard at night. But each time, after she had stared hard for a while, the pictures would vanish.

Mrs. Zimmermann hardly knew what to think of all this. Perhaps it was some leftover magic of her own, because, after all, she was a witch. Not an evil witch with a broomstick and a hoarse laugh, but a friendly, wrinkly-faced witch with a mop of disorderly gray hair. And she was a witch who loved the color purple instead of black, which was what witches were supposed to wear.

A lot of the things in Mrs. Zimmermann's house were purple: the china clock, the wallpaper, the rugs, the soap in the bathroom, and most of Mrs. Zimmermann's dresses. Her witchery was the kindly and eccentric sort, which was why she really didn't feel that the lights in the parlor and the pictures on the wall belonged to her—a few of them seemed sinister somehow, dark and threatening. Still, maybe they were a reflection of her present state of mind, which was not very cheerful.

The year was 1951. Though Mrs. Zimmermann was only sixty-four, lately there were times when she felt a hundred and two. Being lonely didn't help. Her best friend, Jonathan Barnavelt, who lived in a Victorian mansion next door, was away for the summer. He and his nephew Lewis were in Europe seeing the sights. Jonathan was also a wizard, so he and Mrs. Zimmermann had lots in common. Mrs. Zimmermann could have gone with them, but she had just not felt like it. Perhaps she would have if Rose Rita Pottinger, Lewis's best friend, had taken the trip, as they had all planned. However, Rose Rita had broken her ankle in June, so she was forced to stay home. Mrs. Zimmermann knew how disappointed Rose Rita was about missing the trip, and she simply did not have the heart to go and leave Rose Rita behind in the town of New Zebedee, Michigan.

Despite her injury, Rose Rita did show up at Mrs. Zimmermann's house a lot: Her father drove her, and she would hobble in to play chess and backgammon and talk about this and that. Mrs. Zimmermann was grateful for the company, but still she felt depressed. Depressed and anxious, like someone who was waiting for something awful to happen. What was she waiting for? She would have given a lot to know.

On the eighth evening after the visions began, Mrs. Zimmermann and Rose Rita were sitting in Mrs. Zimmermann's kitchen discussing the odd things that had been happening. Rose Rita was fourteen, and she was tall and gawky. She wore glasses, and her hair was black and stringy. Since she was staying the night, she was wearing her rose-pink pajamas and bathrobe, and every now and then she would reach down, trying to scratch an itch on the ankle with the cast on it.

Mrs. Zimmermann was wrapped in her purple-flowered bathrobe, and she had just lit a cigar in the usual way—by snapping a match out of thin air. A long, leisurely trail of smoke drifted toward the open window. The lined curtains stirred in the night breeze, and moths and other night insects fluttered on the screen.

"So what do you think it all means, Mrs. Zimmermann?" asked Rose Rita with a worried frown. "Is there a ghost loose in your house, or what?"

Mrs. Zimmermann waited a long time before answering. "Not a ghost, exactly," she said slowly. "But I do feel that someone is trying to contact me. And I think I know who that someone may be."

Rose Rita tried again to reach an itchy spot under the cast. It was really driving her crazy tonight. "Who is it?" she asked.

"I think it may be Granny Wetherbee. This feels like her kind of magic."

Rose Rita looked puzzled. "Granny Wetherbee? Who's she?"

Mrs. Zimmermann sighed. "Well, I don't mention her much, but she taught me most of what I know about magic. It's true that I have a Doctor of Magic Arts degree from the University of Göttingen in Germany, but that was just the frosting on the cake. The real magic that I know, I learned from Granny. She was the one who showed me how to find my own powers and how to use them. She was not my real grandmother, but an old woman I met when I was about your age. Of course, Granny Wetherbee is long dead. But for some reason she seems to need to contact me."

"Why?" It seemed like a simplistic question to ask, but Rose Rita had learned that when magic was involved, sometimes the most obvious questions brought the most interesting answers, so she asked it anyway.

"Why, indeed?" muttered Mrs. Zimmermann. "Maybe she wants to restore my magic powers."

Rose Rita made a wry face. "If only she could. Then you could do something about this itchy old cast!"

Mrs. Zimmermann gave Rose Rita a sympathetic smile. "I wish I could help, but as you very well know, my powers were just about wiped out in that battle I had with the evil spirit eighteen months ago."

Rose Rita began to shiver a little. She remembered that battle, all right. Sometimes she still had nightmares about it. But she knew that even without her magic, Mrs. Zimmermann was probably the last person in the world to give in to despair or gloom. "Would you be happier if you could be a witch again?" Rose Rita asked. "I mean a real witch, and not just one who can pull lighted matches out of the air?"

Mrs. Zimmermann said thoughtfully, "Maybe so. Oh, when I lost most of my magic, I thought it wouldn't be so bad. For a while I even managed to convince myself that I was happy. But I have to admit that I haven't been very happy for nearly a whole year now."

"But you do the things you always did. You play cards with Lewis and his uncle Jonathan and me, and you bake wonderful chocolate-chip cookies, and you're one of my best friends."

With a smile, Mrs. Zimmermann said, "I know. I really have no right to complain. But I just have the feeling that something is wrong, somehow. Maybe my life would be better if I had those old powers back. Maybe I'd be more cheerful and optimistic. I had my magic for almost fifty years, which is most of my life. Now that it's gone, somehow I don't know how to live properly anymore. Anyway, if those lights and pictures really are from Granny, I'd like to know more about them."

Rose Rita had a troubled look. Since she had met Mrs. Zimmermann and Jonathan Barnavelt two years ago, she had seen lots of magic, and some of it was nasty and wicked. She traced patterns on the tabletop with her finger, and then finally she spoke. "I like you the way you are, Mrs. Zimmermann," she said suddenly. "And I don't think you should mess around with things that you don't understand. What if it isn't Granny Whosis trying to get in contact with you? What if it's somebody evil? You've told me how hard it is sometimes to tell good magic from evil. You should be careful!"

Mrs. Zimmermann stared for a second, and then she laughed. "Good heavens, Rose Rita!" she exclaimed. "You always say what's on your mind, don't you? But don't you worry. I'm old enough to be your grandmother, and I've seen a lot of things in life that you haven't. No, I can't believe that the lights and pictures are evil. They may be, oh, spooky and gloomy and even scary, but they don't seem to aim any evil *my* way. Anyway, I have a feeling in the pit of my stomach that it's Granny who is trying to contact me."

"But you say the images are scary," Rose Rita said, stubbornly.

"Well, I didn't mean to call them *scary*, exactly. They don't frighten me at all. Oh, it's true that there's something sad about those lights and pictures, but then Granny was a pretty sour old woman. Do not worry about me, Rose Rita. I just have to wait for her to show herself to me more fully—then I'll know what it is that I'm supposed to do."

Rose Rita still looked doubtful, but she knew that there was not much point in trying to argue with Mrs. Zimmermann. She was a very stubborn person, and when she thought she was right, you couldn't budge her. Mrs. Zimmermann talked on about Granny Wetherbee's earth magic, her herbs and roots and divining rods. Meanwhile, Rose Rita stared at the reflection of the overhead lamp in the dark pool of cocoa in her cup. The reflection made her think of a fantastic lighted spaceship hurtling through a black void. Before she knew it, she was nodding and dreaming about outer space, flying saucers, and little green men.

"Good heavens!" Mrs. Zimmermann's exclamation brought Rose Rita awake again. "Just look at the time," Mrs. Zimmermann said. "We should have been in bed hours ago. I'll clear the table. You go brush your teeth."

Still feeling very drowsy, Rose Rita hobbled into the bathroom, where everything was purple, from the medicine cabinet to the toilet paper. She heard Mrs. Zimmermann clattering about in the kitchen. As she brushed her teeth, Rose Rita studied her reflection in the purple-framed mirror. She was a skinny, homely girl, she thought. She still wore jeans and sweatshirts and sneakers most of the time, but sometimes now she felt like dressing up. There were times when she wished she were prettier, and there were other times when she was perfectly satisfied being just who she was. Tonight she could not quite make up her mind, but she did notice that her reflection looked just as sleepy as she felt.

Since the cast on her ankle made climbing stairs difficult, Rose Rita was staying in a downstairs bedroom instead of the upstairs guest room. It was a cozy bedroom next door to the dining room, with a neat little single bed covered by a comforter embroidered with bouquets of violets. On the wall over the bed was a painting of purple water lilies, signed by the French painter Monet. He had given the painting to Mrs. Zimmermann during her visit to France in 1913. Rose Rita had just slipped into bed when Mrs. Zimmermann looked in to make sure she was all right. Rose Rita murmured a quiet "Good night," and she heard Mrs. Zimmermann climb the stairs to her own bedroom. A second later Rose Rita was sound asleep.

But upstairs in her bedroom Mrs. Zimmermann lay

wide awake, staring at the ceiling. The luminous hands of the Westclox alarm clock beside the bed told her it was almost twelve. Mrs. Zimmermann glanced at them from time to time as she lay thinking. She waited until midnight, then swung herself out of bed. She put on her bathrobe and slippers and padded downstairs to the living room.

What she saw made her catch her breath: The flashing lights had never been as bright as they were tonight, and this time they seemed to be coming from an old mirror that hung over a bookcase on one wall. The mirror had a mahogany frame and had never seemed magical—not until now. But it was shooting red and green and white flashes in all directions, and as Mrs. Zimmermann drew closer, she saw a shape floating under the shimmering surface of the glass. It might have been a pale moon or a huge egg or a pinkish plate, but it was none of these things. It was a face.

Mrs. Zimmermann stared, wide-eyed. At first the face was vague and blurred, like something glimpsed at night through a rain-spattered window. The lights flickering over it made it hard to see. But then it got clearer, and Mrs. Zimmermann could tell that it was Granny Wetherbee's face. Granny Wetherbee looked just the way Mrs. Zimmermann remembered from childhood: She had a little wrinkled apple of a face, all lines and hollows. Her cheeks were pink and her pale lips were turned down. Under wispy white eyebrows her black eyes shone brightly from deep sockets. And her mouth was moving.

Inside her brain Mrs. Zimmermann heard Granny's cracked, familiar voice. "Well, Florrie, it's been a long time." Granny Wetherbee was the only one who ever called Mrs. Zimmermann that. She was always "Florence" to her family, "Mrs. Zimmermann" to Rose Rita and Lewis, and "Frizzy Wig," "Pruny Face," and similar nicknames to Jonathan. But Granny Wetherbee had never called her anything but "Florrie." The old voice went on: "Listen to me, Florrie dear. Listen very, very carefully."

The dead woman spoke for some time, telling her friend what she had to do to get her old magic powers back. Mrs. Zimmermann listened and smiled and nodded. Granny Wetherbee's voice went on and on, and Mrs. Zimmermann heard it as it echoed in her mind. After some minutes had passed in this way, the mirror went dark and the flashing lights died.

Mrs. Zimmermann trembled a little and blinked. She stood in the darkened living room and felt as if she had just come out of a dream. Without bothering to turn on the lights, she walked out of the room and began to climb the stairs. She yawned and felt half asleep, but a dreamy smile was on her face. At last she had the answer to her prayers—her life would be renewed.

CHAPTER TWO

For a long time nothing happened. Weeks passed, and Rose Rita got postcards from Jonathan and Lewis. They showed the usual scenes, like the Houses of Parliament in London, the Eiffel Tower in Paris, and St. Peter's in Rome. The travelers meant the cards to be cheerful, but they just made Rose Rita feel depressed. She was sorry she hadn't been able to go with her friends. Worse, she secretly suspected that her broken ankle was the reason that Mrs. Zimmermann had passed up the European trip.

As for Mrs. Zimmermann, she was acting stranger and stranger. Sometimes Rose Rita would get late-night calls from her friend, but Mrs. Zimmermann's conversation was weird and disconnected. Rose Rita just couldn't make much sense out of it. When Rose Rita asked about the nightly visions, Mrs. Zimmermann either fell silent or changed the subject.

Since Mrs. Zimmermann was usually levelheaded and calm, the change alarmed Rose Rita. And whenever Rose Rita went over to Mrs. Zimmermann's house for backgammon or chess or just for conversation, it was not much fun. Mrs. Zimmermann's mind was not on games or on anything else that Rose Rita could understand. It was somewhere far, far away.

In the middle of July Rose Rita's cast came off, and she found that she could limp around pretty well. One evening when she was at Mrs. Zimmermann's house, she saw her friend's old battered leather suitcase sitting in the front hall. It was dusted and clean, ready to be packed.

"Are . . . are you going somewhere, Mrs. Zimmermann?" asked Rose Rita in a faltering tone.

Mrs. Zimmermann gave Rose Rita a startled sidelong glance. "Uh, well . . . yes, you might say so," she muttered. "I, uh, have some business out in Pennsylvania."

Business? What on earth was Mrs. Zimmermann talking about? She had taught school at one time, but she had retired, and she lived on a small but comfortable income. Rose Rita knew that long ago Mrs. Zimmermann had occasionally visited an older sister in Pennsylvania, but the sister had died before the Second World War. Now Mrs. Zimmermann had no relatives left there. More than ever, Rose Rita worried that Mrs. Zimmermann was losing her mind.

They went out to the kitchen and set up the board for backgammon. Mrs. Zimmermann brought out her special chocolate-chip cookies and made iced tea. Soon the two of them were deep in a game. Whenever Jonathan played backgammon or checkers, he used foreign silver and gold coins for counters. Mrs. Zimmermann contented herself with plain old red and black wooden checkers. She and Rose Rita pushed these around on the game board for a while.

After some minutes of biting her lip and keeping her eyes on the game, Rose Rita asked in a strained voice, "When are . . . when are you leaving, Mrs. Zimmermann?" She did not look up from the board.

"The day after tomorrow," said Mrs. Zimmermann calmly. "I have a few more concerns to wrap up around here, and then I'm off."

"Will you be away for very long?" Rose Rita asked.

Mrs. Zimmermann moved one of her red men on the board. "Oh, for ten days or two weeks, probably. I'll be home in time to greet Weird Beard and Lewis when they return in August."

"Weird Beard" was Mrs. Zimmermann's pet name for Jonathan Barnavelt. When Mrs. Zimmermann used the nickname, it was a sign that she was in good spirits.

Rose Rita felt her muscles grow tense, the way they always did when she wanted something very much and was afraid she could not have it. "Mrs. . . . Mrs. Zimmermann?" she said, in a faltering voice. "Can . . . can I go with you?"

The question astonished Mrs. Zimmermann. She hardly knew what to say, and it took her a while to collect her thoughts. Finally, she raised her eyes, and her gaze met Rose Rita's. It was clear that Mrs. Zimmermann wanted company—a companion who would go with her on the long and hazardous journey that lay ahead of her. "If your parents will give you permission," Mrs. Zimmermann said slowly, "I'd love you to come along. But there may be dangers. It may be as bad as our trip to Cousin Oley's farm last summer, when old Gert Bigger nearly turned me into a chicken for life and tried to put you under a death spell. To be fair, I have to warn you beforehand."

Now, some people are worrywarts. Lewis was one of these. He was afraid of practically everything, and even when life was going well, he would dream up non-existent dangers to fret about. It was funny, in a way, because once or twice Lewis had faced real danger with courage. On the other hand, little everyday problems flustered and frightened him.

However, Rose Rita was not like Lewis at all. She saw danger more as a possible adventure than a threat. Despite Mrs. Zimmermann's warning, she remained unruffled. Her level gaze met Mrs. Zimmermann's. "If there's trouble," she said quietly, "I'll share it with you. I'm your friend, through thick and thin."

Mrs. Zimmermann smiled warmly. "To the bitter end! We'll see the bad times out and the good times in. Shake on that, Rose Rita Poet," she said. "Very well! I'll pick you up at eight A.M. sharp the day after tomorrow. Have your bags packed and ready to go. Okay?"

The next day Rose Rita went to work on her parents. It didn't actually take much persuading. Mrs. Pottinger thought that Mrs. Zimmermann was a solid, reliable person. Oh, she acted a bit stern, but that was normal for a retired schoolteacher. Mrs. Zimmermann's no-nonsense air reassured Rose Rita's mother. She knew that her daughter would not do anything rash while under her supervision. And although Mr. Pottinger had been known to call Mrs. Zimmermann "the town screwball," Rose Rita could win her father around with a little pleading.

And besides, as Rose Rita reminded her mother, this little excursion to Pennsylvania would be educational. It also would help make up for the European trip that she had missed because of her accident. And she wouldn't have to put much strain on her weak ankle. It would be a car trip out to Someplace, Pennsylvania, and back again.

Rose Rita's parents thought it over. After telephoning Mrs. Zimmermann for a short conference, they agreed to let her go. In a whirlwind of activity, Rose Rita got ready.

So, the day after that, Rose Rita stood waiting on her front porch with her black valise when Bessie, Mrs. Zimmermann's green 1950 Plymouth, rolled up to the curb.

"Hi, Rose Rita!" called Mrs. Zimmermann, waving from the open car window. "Are you ready to plunge off into the wilds of Pennsylvania with me?"

Rose Rita grinned. This was the old devil-may-care, jaunty Mrs. Zimmermann. The apprehensive, anxious air was gone—everything would be all right. As her mother waved good-bye to her from the porch, Rose Rita stuffed her bag into the humped trunk of Mrs. Zimmermann's car. She climbed in beside Mrs. Zimmermann and noticed a large, flat, rectangular package braced on the backseat. It was wrapped in brown paper and packing tape. "What's that?" Rose Rita asked.

"All in good time," Mrs. Zimmermann responded. "Ready? We're off!" In a cloud of exhaust smoke they roared away.

All that July day they drove slowly through southern Michigan and into a corner of Ohio. Mrs. Zimmermann explained that she was in no real hurry. They would just enjoy the trip as they went along, and so they took their time.

They ate at little roadside cafes and hamburger stands,

and they spent nights in the most unlikely-looking tourist cabins Mrs. Zimmermann could find. Although Mrs. Zimmermann's magic was mostly gone, her witchy sixth sense was still working, because they always found the accommodations good and the food tasty. Some nights they stayed up late listening to Detroit Tiger baseball games on the radio while Mrs. Zimmermann played solitaire.

A couple of times when they unpacked for the night, Rose Rita asked Mrs. Zimmermann about the mysterious package. Mrs. Zimmermann always smiled and winked. "You'll know when it's time" was all she would say. She insisted on handling the wrapped package herself, and she always put it up on the highest shelf in the cabin. Then in the morning she would take it out to the Plymouth without ever letting Rose Rita so much as touch it. Mrs. Zimmermann's mysterious teasing exasperated Rose Rita in a happy sort of way. It was a little like having Christmas packages wrapped and lying in plain sight, with no shaking allowed.

Finally they came to the Cumberland Mountains in Pennsylvania. The Cumberlands are low mountains, covered with trees. Engineers have blasted long tunnels through them, and the tunnels are lined with whirring fans that suck out the exhaust smoke of the cars and trucks roaring through. The tunnels are lighted, of course, which makes them less spooky. Still, Rose Rita was always happy when she saw the glimmering crescent of light at the far end. It meant that another cavern in the mountains was almost past.

The scenery around them began to change. They had been passing farms the whole way, but the farms of Ohio were like the ones in Michigan. Most of them grew corn and wheat, and tractors hummed out in the fields. The barns were red and steep roofed, and on their sides they bore painted advertisments for things like Mail Pouch Chewing Tobacco. Once they reached the Cumberland Mountains of Pennsylvania, they drove past smaller farms with huge red barns that often had odd bright-colored decorations painted on their sides. These were usually circles, and in the circles were teardrops, five-pointed stars, hearts, flowers, or staring eyes. Mrs. Zimmermann explained that these were hex signs.

Some Pennsylvania farmers were superstitious. Barns with seven hex signs painted on their sides supposedly warded off bad luck, like lightning or fire, and the evil spells of witches. Rose Rita wanted to know more. When they stopped for the night, she asked Mrs. Zimmermann to tell her about the farmers and their beliefs.

It was the fourth evening of their trip. Rose Rita and Mrs. Zimmermann were staying at Deutschmacher's Motel in the middle of the Cumberland Mountains. It was a starry night, and the mountains were great, dark, shadowy shapes on all sides. As they sat on the screened porch of their cabin, Mrs. Zimmermann talked about the Pennsylvania Dutch. "Don't let the name fool you," she said. "They are really Germans."

"Then why are they called Dutch?" Rose Rita asked, knowing that Mrs. Zimmermann expected the question.

"The mistake occurred more than two centuries ago," Mrs. Zimmermann explained. "Lots of German settlers came to Pennsylvania because it offered religious tolerance. They knew that much, although they didn't know any English. The non-German frontiersmen knew only that their neighbors spoke a language they couldn't understand. They misinterpreted the word *Deutsch*, which means "German." The best that English tongues could do with such a strange word was *Dutch*, and so that is what they called the Germans. Anyway, the mistake stuck, and people call them the Pennsylvania Dutch to this day. They have their own folkways and superstitions and beliefs, like most close-knit groups. You'll meet a few of them before this trip is over."

She went on to talk about Pennsylvania Dutch witch beliefs, about *hexerei*, or evil magic. Hex witches, male and female, often put enemies under curses, and sometimes the curses killed the victims. Mrs. Zimmermann explained that the first witch trial in Pennsylvania had occurred in 1683, when a Philadelphia court found a woman named Margaret Mattson not guilty of being a hex witch. The most recent one, she said, had taken place just two years ago, in 1949.

She chatted away for most of an hour. These days,

that was a long speech for Mrs. Zimmermann. Rose Rita was comforted by her friend's display of useless knowledge, but later that evening she began again to feel anxious. Toward ten o'clock Mrs. Zimmermann started acting odd again. The mirrors in the tourist cabin appeared to fascinate her, and she peered into them as if she expected to see secrets hidden there. And more and more her eyes had that faraway look, as if she were seeing faces or landscapes or shapes that no one else could see.

Tonight they were playing chess, but it wasn't much fun, because Mrs. Zimmermann kept making stupid mistakes. In one game she gave her queen away for no reason at all. In another she conceded because she was two pawns and a knight behind. Usually Mrs. Zimmermann would fight to the bitter end, but tonight her playing was listless and mechanical. And every now and then a noise outside would startle her, and she would get up and rush out onto the front steps of the cabin. After looking wildly in all directions, she would come back, cough in an embarrassed way, and start playing chess again.

These strange actions frightened Rose Rita, and more than ever she began to feel that something bad was going to happen. But whatever this something was, it remained hidden to her. Mrs. Zimmermann simply shrugged off all her questions. Rose Rita had to sit and wait.

The next morning the two travelers had a big Penn

Dutch breakfast in the motel's dining room: pancakes and syrup and fat German sausages. Mrs. Zimmermann paid the bill. Then the two of them threw their bags into the car, Mrs. Zimmermann carefully replaced the mysterious package, and they were on the road again. They rambled slowly from one small town to another. In the afternoon Mrs. Zimmermann found a baseball game on the car radio. The Boston Red Sox were playing the Cleveland Indians. Every time the car went through a tunnel, the sound faded out, and there were a lot of tunnels. Rose Rita didn't like them at all. She could not keep her mind on the game, even though it was an exciting one. The teams were tied 4–4, and the hard-fought contest went on and on through extra innings. Finally, in the sixteenth inning, Boston loaded the bases. Just as Clyde Vollmer came up to bat for the Sox, another tunnel loomed ahead. This one looked darker and more sinister than the rest. The painted sign over the stone arch said that the tunnel was one and one tenth miles long. To Rose Rita the entrance of the tunnel was forbidding—it might as well have been the yawning mouth of a tomb. She felt a tight knot in her stomach as Mrs. Zimmermann steered the car in with a weird smile on her face. The radio lost the signal, and the sound whispered away to static. On they drove, as the exhaust fans whirred overhead and the fluorescent lights pointed the way.

Finally a glimmering light showed in the distance,

and Rose Rita began to breathe more easily. Then, as they got closer to the other end of the tunnel, she began to realize that something was wrong—very wrong. The light was too bright and too white to be the ordinary sunlight of an ordinary July day. And then they burst out into a landscape of winter.

Icicles hung from all the trees, and heavy snow covered all the mountains. The Plymouth crunched into a snowbank that was surely knee-deep. In a long, shivering jolt the car stopped dead still. With terror clutching her heart, Rose Rita looked behind her.

Running along the cliff base, and stretching out before them, was a glittering, slippery, snow-covered track. It wound down the hillside ahead. It looked unpaved and was far too narrow to be called a road. Worst of all, the tunnel behind them had completely disappeared. There was only the forbidding, pitted stone face of the cliff. It was solid and unbroken, as if the tunnel had never existed at all.

They were marooned in a strange enchanted world, a world that Rose Rita could not understand, a world where she instinctively felt that anything might happen.

CHAPTER THREE

With the Plymouth's hood embedded in the snowbank, the engine sputtered and died, and for a few seconds all was silent. At a loss for words, Rose Rita looked around again at a landscape that was unquestionably pretty, but that was completely out of place. The day was hazy bright. The sun shone wanly through a high, icy layer of cloud, and the light reflected off the icicles and the drifts of snow. Then Mrs. Zimmermann said briskly, "Well, I certainly didn't expect *this*! I only hope my poor car has survived the shock of going tobogganing."

Rose Rita stared at her friend in wonder. Didn't Mrs. Zimmermann see what a mess they were in? Already the air inside the car felt chilly. The modern paved highway they had been driving on had vanished, and in its place was a country lane, narrow and unpaved and coated with ice. Yet Mrs. Zimmermann made a joke of their accident. She sounded as unconcerned as if they had only taken a wrong turn or if the car had blown a tire. Maybe Mrs. Zimmermann had really gone out of her mind. Rose Rita felt frightened, but she wasn't the sort of person who usually panicked. For some reason Mrs. Zimmermann's little jest really irritated her. She cried out, "Mrs. Zimmermann, this is *weird.* It's scary, not some kind of funny story! Get us out of here!"

After one startled glance Mrs. Zimmermann gave her a friendly pat on the shoulder and a reassuring smile, although it looked forced and strained. "Come on, Rose Rita. You've seen me fool around with magic enough to take in stride something as minor as an unscheduled change of weather. I'll admit that finding a tunnel into the middle of winter isn't an ordinary, everyday occurrence, but then neither is this an ordinary, everyday trip. We're out looking for magic. Let me set Bessie to rights, and then I'll explain what I think has happened to us."

She carefully started the Plymouth's engine and then eased the car into reverse. As the engine raced, the wheels spun with a high whirring noise and the car rocked back and forth, but the hood did not budge from the snowbank. "Hmpf!" said Mrs. Zimmermann. "We need more traction. Let's see what we can do." They got out of the car. Mrs. Zimmermann stooped low to look at the rear wheels. Then she pointed to the side of the road, where piles of dead tree branches lay in a tangle under the shelter of the roadside firs. "Let's get some of those and shove them under the rear tires. I once saw Jonathan get his antique car out of a similar predicament that way."

Already Rose Rita was shivering, and her teeth chattered from the cold, but being active helped her warm up a little. She trotted back and forth, helping Mrs. Zimmermann drag two dozen small branches across the road. Then they jammed the branches under the rear tires. Mrs. Zimmermann nodded and said, "That ought to do it. Let's try again now."

The car felt warm after the icy chill outside. Mrs. Zimmermann started the engine and again put the car into reverse, but this time she was careful to apply the gas gradually. Bessie slowly began to move, crunching over the dead wood with a loud crackling sound. Once the car had moved over the branches, it hesitated for a moment. Rose Rita caught her breath. She was afraid the car would slip back down the hill. Then the rear tires got a better grip on the icy surface and pulled them back onto the lane as a few clumps of snow fell from the fenders, front bumper, and grille.

"Very good," Mrs. Zimmermann said, sounding relieved. "Now we have to get to the bottom of the hill in one piece. And I think we'll turn on the heater too."

The path in front of them led downward, not very steeply, but it wound as it descended the hill. The Plymouth edged forward slowly, and they passed the flattened black tree branches and the gouge in the snowbank that the hood had made. The engine was already warm and the heater began to blow toasty air against their legs. With a little sigh of contentment Mrs. Zimmermann said, "There! Now let's see if we can get to civilization, and once we're safe, I'll tell you where and when we are."

"*When* we are?" Rose Rita asked. The phrase did not exactly throw her, because she had read about time travel before, in H. G. Wells's *The Time Machine*. She immediately grasped what Mrs. Zimmermann was implying, although she could not believe it. "You mean we're in a different year?"

"Do you think this is 1951?" Mrs. Zimmermann said tensely as she tried to guide the automobile down the icy hillside. She had a little frown of concentration on her face, and her hands gripped the steering wheel tightly. The Plymouth had picked up speed. Then all at once it began to swerve in an unpleasant way. As the tires slipped, Mrs. Zimmermann spun the wheel first one way and then the other, and then she said, "Whoops—hold on!"

The car had gone into a downhill skid. Bessie slipped right off the left side of the lane with a tooth-rattling bounce and kept going. It felt like a ride on the Alpine

Adventure, the roller-coaster that came to the New Zebedee athletic fields with the Capharnaum County Agricultural Fair every fall. Rose Rita didn't quite close her eyes as the car plowed into a dense, snowheaped clump of rhododendron with a scrape of branches on metal. Abruptly they plunged from thin wintry sunlight into spooky, silent darkness as the car skidded into the very center of the thicket. For a second time the engine coughed, clattered, and died.

"Well!" Mrs. Zimmermann said. "That's *it*, as far I'm concerned. Driving on ice is far from my favorite thing to do. And since I don't have any chains in the trunk, I suppose we'll have to wait until the ice thaws."

"Wait? Here?" Rose Rita asked. "We'll freeze to death!"

Mrs. Zimmermann clicked her tongue. "No, we certainly can't wait in the car for someone to rescue us. I doubt that anyone could even see us from the road. But we're fairly close to the town of Stonebridge, unless we've moved in space as well as time. I don't think we have, because this scenery looks very familiar. From our surroundings, I would say we must be in, oh, about 1898 or 1900 or so."

Rose Rita could not help feeling distraught. "I don't know what you're talking about or how you got that time travel idea. All I can see is that we left summer and now it's winter. And the car is stuck, and we don't have any way out, and it's getting cold."

"Good heavens, Rose Rita!" Mrs. Zimmermann reflected that Rose Rita really had a legitimate complaint. After all, though she had warned Rose Rita that the trip might involve danger, she had not specified what type of danger to expect. And even though Rose Rita did have some reason to anticipate something odd, going from summer into winter did call for some explanation. "Listen, and I'll tell you what I think has happened," Mrs. Zimmermann said. "I believe the ghost of Granny Wetherbee has taken us back to the time and place where I first met her. Let me see, my older sister Anna married Harold Crippen in June of 1898, and they moved to Stonebridge, Pennsylvania, where he began his law practice. I visited them that first summer. That was when I met Granny Wetherbee. She was about eighty, and I was almost twelve. After that I often visited my sister and brother-in-law, and during my visits to Stonebridge, Granny Wetherbee taught me about magic."

Rose Rita understood. "So that's where we are now? Near your sister's home?"

Mrs. Zimmermann nodded. "Yes. In 1951 the highway we were on goes through the tunnel, turns south, and runs right through the center of the town. In 1898 it was the Mount Kidron Road. That was an old dirt road which ended on the graveled highway leading into Stonebridge. Unless I'm mistaken, we're on Fuller's Hill. I ought to recognize it, because this is where Otto Pennybaker used to take me sledding. Otto was sort of my first boyfriend, but not really—the two of us were a lot like you and Lewis, I suppose."

Rose Rita blushed. "Lewis is just a boy who happens to be my friend," she said. "He's not my boyfriend. He wouldn't even dance with me. . . ."

Mrs. Zimmermann waited, but Rose Rita did not say anything more about Lewis. "I thought you two were having some kind of problem before Jonathan whisked him away on the European jaunt," she said. "Do you want to talk about it?"

"No," Rose Rita said. "I want to know why you think we're in 1898 and not in 1951."

"Heavens, but you're crabby today. Well, as I was telling you, the reason is simply that it *looks* like 1898 and not like 1951. I haven't been to Stonebridge in years, because my sister died in 1939. Still, even back then the tunnel led through the mountain, and this was a paved road instead of just a wagon track. Now, however, it looks just the way I remember it looking when I was twelve." With a smile Mrs. Zimmermann went on, "Anyway, if this is really the Mount Kidron Road, we must be about four miles from Stonebridge. It won't be a very comfortable walk in this weather, but I think we can make it. And there ought to be some traffic on the Stonebridge Road, even if it is the middle of winter."

Rose Rita's head whirled. "But if we're in 1898, I haven't even been born yet," she said. She did a little subtraction in her head and added, "I won't be born for another thirty-nine years. How can I exist before I was even born?"

"There are some questions I can't answer. As for going back in time, it obviously doesn't affect you physically. I mean, I don't look as if I've gone back to being twelve years old, do I?" Mrs. Zimmermann replied. "Look, Rose Rita, I'm not exactly sure how the magic has worked, and I'm not even sure what I'm supposed to do next. But Granny Wetherbee's ghost told me that to get my powers back, I would have to go back to the beginning place. Those were her very words: 'Florrie, you must return to the beginning place. You must set right the great wrong.' Now, exactly what she meant I can't tell you. She certainly didn't say anything about any 'great wrong' the first time I met her—although she had had an unhappy life. Anyway, we won't find out anything by sitting in the car. You didn't pack any kind of coat, did you?"

Rose Rita shook her head. "No. Only jeans and shirts and a couple of sweatshirts."

Mrs. Zimmermann thought for a moment. "Well . . . that's really pretty good. I have my raincoat and my robe and pajamas. We ought to manage to survive the cold if we each put on several layers of clothes."

The car had made a sort of tunnel into the rhododendron thicket, and branches jammed Rose Rita's door shut, so both of them had to struggle out the driver's door. The disturbed limbs overhead showered down freezing snow that somehow managed to find its way right down their collars. Although the day was bright with the hazy sun, the air outside was bitter, stinging Rose Rita's nose, and beneath the rhododendrons very little sun leaked through. They had no way of judging the temperature, but Rose Rita thought it must be below zero. Fortunately no wind was blowing.

Mrs. Zimmermann opened the trunk, and they began to unpack clothes. Hurrying because of the cold, Rose Rita put on three pairs of jeans, although the last pair had to stay unfastened. She also wore two shirts and two sweatshirts. She had been wearing a pair of brown penny loafers, but at Mrs. Zimmermann's suggestion she took these off and replaced them with her P.F. Flyers sneakers. Since they were nearly new, the treads on the bottoms would give her better traction for walking on ice. She wore two pairs of socks, so the tennis shoes were a tight fit. Finally, as she was about to close her valise, she remembered something she had packed just on a whim. She rummaged until she found it and took it out. It was her old black-plush beanie, decorated with buttons of Kellogg's cereal cartoon characters. She had not worn it in nearly two years. Now, however, she jammed it onto her head, grateful for its added warmth.

Mrs. Zimmermann bundled up similarly, putting on three purple dresses and her purple floral bathrobe and topping off her outfit with her purple raincoat. Although she had packed no sneakers, her regular shoes were good sensible footwear for walking, and she borrowed a couple of pairs of socks from Rose Rita to help keep her feet warm. At one of the stops they had made, Mrs. Zimmermann had bought a souvenir towel decorated with a print of the Toledo city skyline at sunset. She tied the towel around her head as if it were a scarf. She was an odd sight when she had finished, because normally she was quite thin—a slim, upright woman with an untidy mop of frizzy gray hair. With the layers of clothing she now wore, she looked as if she had gained thirty pounds, and Rose Rita had to giggle a little.

Mrs. Zimmermann grinned and stuck out her tongue. "You won't win any fashion prizes either," she said, "but at least we won't freeze solid. All set? Let's see if we can't cover some ground." She slammed the trunk shut with a crash that shook a miniature avalanche off the rhododendron leaves overhead.

They had to help each other over the slippery spots, but both of them were good walkers. Even with Rose Rita limping, they moved along at a fairly fast clip. Rose Rita's beanie helped keep her head warm, and her long hair covered her ears and provided some protection from the frigid air. Mrs. Zimmermann's nose and cheeks soon began to glow a bright red from the cold, and before long both of them were huffing out clouds of vapor, their lungs heaving from exertion.

After five minutes of slippery walking, they came to the bottom of the hill. There a slightly larger road joined the lane they were on. Mrs. Zimmermann paused here, with her hands on her hips. "Now, that's strange," she said. "This must be Fuller's Hill, and I distinctly remember—Oh, never mind."

Rose Rita did mind. "What is it?" she asked, alarmed again. "What's wrong now?"

Mrs. Zimmermann shrugged. "It's probably nothing but my memory playing tricks on me. This should be the Stonebridge Road, but I remember it as being wider and graveled, and there also was a little country store here where the roads come together. At least I think there was. Of course, all this was more than fifty years ago, so I may just be wrong. Well, we'll soon know. Stonebridge is this way."

They turned south onto the new road, which appeared to be more heavily traveled than the road from Fuller's Hill. At least the surface lay rutted down to frozen earth, without a slick, slippery coating of ice. However, although the footing was better, the day was still icy and raw, and Rose Rita became increasingly uncomfortable. Her weak ankle throbbed painfully, her nose began to run, and her chest ached from the cold air. Rose Rita was rarely sick, but regularly once every winter she came down with the sniffles, usually just after the first really cold spell. Now, as they walked along the road, she had the miserable feeling that she was going to get a cold.

Suddenly Mrs. Zimmermann stopped ahead of her,

and Rose Rita almost ran into her. "What is it?"

"Listen," Mrs. Zimmermann said, holding one hand up for silence. From the distance there came a faint jingling, creaking, clopping sound, like a horse and wagon. Rose Rita recognized the sound because her uncle drove a wagon pulled by a team of mules on his farm outside New Zebedee, and she often rode around the farm in the wagon, sometimes even holding the reins. Mrs. Zimmermann turned. "It's coming from that way."

The two travelers paused, looking back along the road, which made a gentle sweeping curve around the foot of Fuller's Hill, and sure enough, after a moment a handsome chestnut-colored horse came into view, stepping high. He was pulling a small green cart that held a man and a child, both of them heavily bundled.

The man gave Mrs. Zimmermann and Rose Rita a long look, and as the cart came up close to them, he reined in the horse. "Whoa, Nicklaus," he said in a deep voice. "Are you in some kind of trouble?" He had a lilting German accent, like Pastor Bunsen at the Grace Lutheran Church back in New Zebedee. The man wore a wide-brimmed black hat, and when he lifted it, he revealed a broad, red face, bright-blue eyes, and an abundance of golden curls just touched with a few streaks of gray. He looked like a man of good humor and goodwill.

"I'm afraid we are," Mrs. Zimmermann said. "Tell me, is this the road to Stonebridge?"

The man formed the word silently with his lips. Then he said it aloud. "Stonebridge. Stonebridge. If you mean Steinbrücke, *ja*, the village is about three miles ahead, but no one calls it Stonebridge." He put his hat back on.

The child beside him had been sitting huddled up, her features concealed by a bonnet and a heavy blanket that wrapped around her shoulders. Now she raised her head. Rose Rita saw that it was a little blond girl a year or two younger than she was, with a plump round face and wide eyes with irises so dark blue they looked black. Beside Rose Rita, Mrs. Zimmermann stiffened. "My God!" she said under her breath. In a louder voice that shook just a little, she repeated to the man, "I'm afraid that we are in trouble. We've lost our ca—our carriage and our way. We need your help, if you don't mind."

"Mind? No, of course not. I will be glad to help in any way. Look, we are much closer to my farm than to Steinbrücke, and it is a very cold day. You get into the cart and I will take you to the farm. My wife and I will give you a good hot meal and beds for the night. In the morning we will see what we can do to help you."

"It's very kind of you to take the trouble," Mrs. Zimmermann said, already climbing into the cart.

"Oh, it is no trouble. Let me give you a hand up, young fellow," the man said to Rose Rita. She realized with embarrassment that he thought she was a boy, probably because of the jeans she wore and the way all those clothes padded her out. She grabbed the man's gloved hand, put one foot on the little metal step, then scrambled up and got into the cart behind the girl, who turned and gave her a shy smile. Mrs. Zimmermann sat on the hard bench beside Rose Rita, staring intently at the child. Their rescuer shook the reins and clicked his tongue, and Nicklaus the horse began to pace along again, his hoofs drumming on the frozen road.

At last Mrs. Zimmermann stirred. "We haven't introduced ourselves. I'm Mrs. Florence Zimmermann. And this young *fellow* is Rose Rita Pottinger. She is, ah, my grand-niece."

The man turned and gave Rose Rita a closer look. "Well, you don't say. So he is a she, eh? I am sorry for the mistake, Miss Rose Rita. My name is Hermann Weiss, and this lady beside me is my daughter, Hilda. You will find a spare blanket folded beneath the seat. Wrap yourselves in it if you are cold."

For a second time Rose Rita felt Mrs. Zimmermann start. Rose Rita was very cold, so she pulled the blanket out and gave one end of it to Mrs. Zimmermann. As if she were in a trance, Mrs. Zimmermann numbly took the blanket and wrapped it around herself. Rose Rita draped the other end around her own shoulders and snuggled close, grateful for the warmth the blanket gave her stiff fingers. She wondered why Mrs. Zimmermann was acting so strangely, and why she stared so hard at the little girl on the seat ahead of them. In fact Rose Rita was burning with questions, but she sensed it would be unwise to ask them in the presence of Mr. Weiss and his daughter. With a sigh that puffed away in a wisp of steamy mist, she realized she would just have to wait.

The truth was that Mrs. Zimmermann had experienced two strong shocks. The first one happened the moment she saw Hilda Weiss, because she immediately recognized the little girl's features. She had seen Hilda's face before. It had been one of the mysterious visions that had flickered across the wall of the passageway outside the pantry. This was the sad little beckoning girl whom she remembered seeing in her own house. And it was possible, though Mrs. Zimmermann was not certain, that Mr. Weiss was one of the laughing people she had seen at another time in the same place. There remained the desolate cemetery at night, but Mrs. Zimmermann was in no hurry to see that vision in real life.

The second shock came when Mrs. Zimmermann heard the girl's name. Granny Wetherbee's full name had been Mrs. Hilda Weiss Wetherbee. The eighty-two-year-old woman Mrs. Zimmermann had once known and this twelve-year-old girl were one and the same.

That explained why there was no country store at the foot of Fuller's Hill—Mrs. Zimmermann and Rose Rita were not in 1898 after all. They had to be in a much, much earlier time. And maybe they were stuck there.

CHAPTER FOUR

Before the cart had gone very far, Hermann Weiss muttered, "Uh-oh. Here comes old Adolphus Stoltzfuss." He sounded both worried and annoyed, and his black-gloved hands tightened their grip on the horse's reins.

Another horse-drawn vehicle was approaching: a farm wagon painted a cheerful, bright yellow. Piled high in the wagon bed were bulging burlap sacks, stuffed full and looking like fat brown pillows. The man driving the wagon was about seventy, tall and skinny, and the horse that drew the wagon was a deep-chested white mare whose ribs showed through the skin. Mr. Weiss edged the cart over to the right as far as he could. The wagon swung wide to pass them. The scowling wagon driver glared their way, shaking his long, bony chin at them. As the two drivers came side by side, the old man in the wagon raised his fist and growled, "Why don't you get that witch out of the country!" Then he added something that sounded to Rose Rita like *"Du ferdammt hess!"*

Mr. Weiss stared straight ahead and did not reply, but his jaw clenched and his hands trembled as they held the reins. A moment later the wagon had safely passed, and Mr. Weiss shook the reins and clicked his tongue. "Get up, Nicklaus," he said. "We will be late for supper." The chestnut horse picked up his pace, and the cart rattled along at a good clip.

The exchange astonished Rose Rita. How in the world had the skinny man known that Mrs. Zimmermann was a witch? No one could tell by looking at her. She certainly didn't look anything like a storybook witch, with a pointed black hat and a tattered black cane and a scraggly broom. Huddled beneath the brown blanket, she might have been just about anyone or anything, but the man had told Weiss to get that witch out of the country. As far as Rose Rita could see, the witch had to be her friend.

Before long, Mr. Weiss pointed ahead to an enormous rock off to the left of the road. It was a snow-streaked chunk of granite the size of a small house. "That is Cottage Rock," he said. "It is on my land. We turn for the house there." Just past the rock the cart swerved off to the left, onto a little-used path with only a couple of wagon ruts showing through the crusted snow. "Not far now," Mr. Weiss said over his shoulder. Rose Rita thought that his voice was no longer light and pleasant, but heavy and sorrowful. She wondered if what the other driver had said about Mrs. Zimmermann had upset him. Though she accepted Mrs. Zimmermann's magic as just part of her friend's life, she knew many people were strongly prejudiced against witches of all types. She began to be afraid that the Weiss family would change its mind about giving them a meal, and she dreaded the thought of walking any farther through the snow.

Soon farm buildings appeared ahead of them, beyond a wide, snow-covered lawn studded with bare chestnut trees. Rose Rita saw a white-plastered house, two stories tall and with two wings, and behind it a barn that was stone for the first story and red-painted wood for the second. Unlike many of the barns in the area, this one bore no hex signs on its red wooden sides. To the right of the barn were a few other outbuildings and sheds, and the cart headed for one of these. Mr. Weiss halted Nicklaus before a broad stable door and turned to his daughter. "Hilda, I will put up the horse and feed him. You take our visitors in to see Mama and tell her we will have guests tonight."

For the first time Hilda spoke: "All right, Papa." She

had a very clear and sweet voice, and her German accent was not as pronounced as her father's. She climbed down and waited while Rose Rita and Mrs. Zimmermann descended from the wagon. "This way," she said. She kept stealing shy glances at Rose Rita. "Are you English?" she asked in little more than a whisper.

"What?" Rose Rita asked, surprised. "Do I sound English?"

Mrs. Zimmermann laughed. "Hilda wants to know if you're one of her people. They call anyone who isn't Pennsylvania Dutch 'English.' By that definition I suppose you'd say that both of us are English. Hilda, we come from a small town called New Zebedee, a long, long way from here."

"Do the girls in this place all wear trousers?" Hilda asked, stealing another look at Rose Rita's attire.

Rose Rita blushed. "They do if they want to," she said. "Anyway, wearing jeans is a lot more comfortable in cold weather."

They had reached a back door to the house. Hilda scraped her shoes and stamped off loose snow, and then she led them inside. At first Rose Rita could hardly see, because even the weak sunlight outside had reflected off the snow so brightly that everything inside was dark by comparison. To complicate matters, her glasses fogged up. In the dimness an impression of warmth and bustle swept over her. She could tell from the chatter that they had entered a house with lots of people in it. After a moment a child yelled, "Mama! Hilda has brought strangers in!"

Rose Rita took off her spectacles and used the hem of her sweatshirt to rub the mist from them. She put the glasses back on and blinked. A portly woman came bustling in, drying her hands on a towel. "Hilda, you look half frozen! Who are these you've brought in? What is your papa doing? How was Lawyer Nuttenhaus? What did he say about Grampa Drexel? Are your boots wet? Does it look as if it will snow again?"

Hilda picked out just one question to answer. She said, "Mama, this is Mrs. Florence Zimmermann and Miss Rose Rita Pottinger. Papa and I found them walking on the road. They've lost their way. Papa says they're to have supper with us and stay here tonight."

Mrs. Weiss put both hands to her head. "Chatter, chatter, chatter! *Ach*, child, you'll make my head break with all your talking one day. But if we have guests, then we must make ready for them. Hilda, go and mind the stew and tell Sarah to put two more plates on the table. Hurry, now!"

Hilda gave Mrs. Zimmermann and Rose Rita a parting smile and went through the doorway from which Mrs. Weiss had emerged. Mrs. Weiss tucked a loose strand of her gray-blond hair back into place and smiled. "Hello, Mrs. Zimmermann. I am Susanna Weiss. Are you related to the Hanover Zimmermanns? No, of course, they are all Amish, aren't they? Lost, were you? How dreadful, and the weather so terribly cold too! Have you ever seen more unsettled weather so late in February? *Ach*, we have had troubles this year, I don't mind telling you! Never mind, though—you are welcome. And is Rose Rita your granddaughter, then? I have two daughters about her age or a little older, twins, and their names are Rebecca and Sarah."

"Rose Rita is my grand-niece," said Mrs. Zimmermann, who had decided that Hilda's approach of answering just one of Mrs. Weiss's inquiries might be the best one. "Actually, she's sort of my adopted grand-niece."

"How nice," Mrs. Weiss said. "You know, my stepfather lives with us, Grampa Drexel. *Ach*, how the poor old fellow has suffered. He has not been well at all this whole winter. My mother's second husband he was, but to me a loving father nevertheless. My own father died when I was only two, so I do not even remember him. God bless him, Mr. Drexel has always been just like a papa to me. Poor man, he does not deserve all this trouble and worry. I hope you both like hot mummix? It's plain fare, but we have plenty of it, and it will warm you on such a cold day. Papa, here you are!"

Mr. Weiss had come inside and stood behind Mrs. Zimmermann and Rose Rita. He took off his wide-brimmed hat and hung it on a peg. He embraced Mrs. Weiss and gave her a quick peck on the cheek. "I hope supper is almost ready," he said. "It's a cold ride from Lawyer Nuttenhaus's place."

"Papa?" asked Mrs. Weiss.

Mr. Weiss made a sad face and then shook his head. Mrs. Weiss sighed deeply. Rose Rita felt puzzled. For a woman who used so many words, Mrs. Weiss seemed to get a world of meaning from a shake of the head.

With another sigh Mrs. Weiss turned to her two visitors. In a more subdued voice she said, "Mrs. Zimmermann, there is hot water in the washroom beside the kitchen. You and your niece can wash your hands and faces there. Come, I'll show you."

They went through the kitchen, where what seemed like a dozen children swarmed all over the place. Some ofthem were putting wood into a cast-iron stove, some were stirring pots, and others were running back and forth with hands full of dishes or silverware. One boy paused and stared hard at Rose Rita. "*Ach!*" he said timidly. "What a wonderful hat she has!"

Rose Rita had forgotten the beanie. She snatched it off her head and stuffed it under her topmost sweatshirt. Then she followed Mrs. Zimmermann to the washroom. After the bustle of the kitchen, the dark little room behind the stove was quiet by comparison. Mrs. Weiss poured some hot water into a basin, gave Mrs. Zimmermann a plain towel, and then hurried back into the kitchen. As soon as she was out of earshot, Rose Rita said, "Mrs. Zimmermann, how did that man on the road, that Adolphus Whosis, know that you were a witch?"

Mrs. Zimmermann took off her improvised scarf. "I don't think he meant me. I think the Weisses are having witch troubles of another kind. Here, you can dry your hands on Toledo. I'll use the linen towel myself."

Rose Rita took the towel and wiped her hands. "What kind of witch troubles?"

"I'll tell you later," Mrs. Zimmermann replied. "Let's go in to supper. I'm starved."

Rose Rita was not hungry. Not after the shock of all she had been through that day. And especially not for something called *mummix*, which sounded strange and rather Egyptian to her. But because she did not know what else to do, she seated herself on one of the long wooden benches drawn up to the heavily laden table. The Weiss children already sat on that bench and the one across the long table.

The children's names were hard to keep straight. Rose Rita sat between Rebecca, who was sixteen, and Hilda. On the far side of Rebecca was Sarah, her identical twin. Across from them was Heinrich, a pale and skinny ten-year-old whose look of apprehension reminded Rose Rita of her chubby friend Lewis. Heinrich was the one who had been so visibly impressed by her beanie. Two older boys sat beside Heinrich. Their names were Hans and Jacob, but Rose Rita could not remember who was who.

Mrs. Zimmermann was on the other side of Hilda. Mrs. Weiss sat next to her. Mr. Weiss disappeared for a few moments, and then he came back with an elderly man leaning on his arm.

The old man looked frail, but his blue eyes were bright. He was thin and unsteady on his legs. Once Mr. Weiss had seen him into a chair at the foot of the table, he said, "This is Grampa Drexel, my wife's stepfather. Grampa Drexel, these are our guests, Mrs. Zimmermann and her grand-niece Rose Rita." Grampa Drexel smiled at both of them and gave them a courteous nod, but when he gave Mrs. Zimmermann a second look, he seemed startled. Rose Rita noticed that the old man kept glancing back at her with a suspicious look in his eyes.

Mr. Weiss took his place at the head of the table and said a long grace. By the time he had finished, Rose Rita had changed her mind about not being hungry. Mummix turned out to be a sort of beef stew with potatoes, piping hot and savory. Mrs. Weiss also served a hot cabbage slaw, buttered peas, freshly-baked brown bread with fresh creamy butter, and fat, brown apple dumplings. Rose Rita ate just as heartily as the girls on either side of her.

Near the end of the meal one of the older boys said, "Papa, what about the lawyer?"

Mr. Weiss shook his head. "Not now, Hans. We do not wish to discuss our troubles in front of guests. Mrs. Zimmermann, I'm glad we could help you. How did you come to be in such a predicament? Not many people travel the Mount Kidron Road in the wintertime."

Mrs. Zimmermann coughed into her napkin. "I suppose that is true, but we are strangers here and didn't know that. We come from a good way west of here. Rose Rita and I wanted to, ah, look up some of my relatives in the Cumberland Valley, but we had a bit of an accident."

"No wonder," Mrs. Weiss said. "*Ach*, that road is treacherous when it freezes. I remember one time when Reverend Helmholtz—you remember Josef Helmholtz, Hermann, who took Pastor Brunning's place that winter? Anyway, his horse slipped and the poor man fell and broke his leg. Two miles he had to crawl before he found someone to help him."

Grampa Drexel spoke up for the first time, in a kindly but weak voice: "Susanna, let our visitor finish, please."

Mrs. Weiss blushed even pinker than she had been. "I am sorry, Papa Drexel. I know I talk too much."

"No, not at all," Mrs. Zimmermann said. She was glad for the diversion. She had no idea of how to explain an automobile accident to these people who had never seen a gasoline engine.

"Was it a bad accident?" young Heinrich asked Rose Rita.

"Well, our, uh, carriage ran off the road," Rose Rita said. "We were coming downhill and the curve was really icy, so we sort of slipped."

Rebecca looked at her with wide eyes. "What happened to your horse?" she asked.

Rose Rita suddenly noticed that she had everyone's attention. She prided herself on her imagination. Now she set it free. "Well, it's a funny thing about that horse," she said. "He was in a bad accident once before, and he had to stay in his stall for months and months. Now whenever there's even a little accident, he thinks he's hurt and he hides and won't move."

"You left him in the *snow*?" Hilda asked, in a shocked voice.

"Uh, no," Rose Rita said. "I mean, he always runs back to the stable at home and hides there. And then we have to bring him his oats on a tray every morning until he feels well enough to come outside again. He—"

Rose Rita broke off. They were all staring at her, and Mrs. Zimmermann was making little "no-no" gestures with her head. Only Mr. Drexel, at the foot of the table, was smiling in an understanding way. He cleared his throat, and everyone looked his way. "I believe I know what the young lady means," he said, and he touched his forehead with a bony finger.

Rose Rita looked down and felt her face go hot. Grampa Drexel was telling everyone she was "touched"! Fortunately Mrs. Weiss broke in with a long comment about the unusually harsh winter, and soon the conversation moved on to other subjects.

After dinner Rose Rita and Mrs. Zimmermann insisted on helping the Weisses clean up. In turn, Mr. and Mrs. Weiss insisted that they both stay with them as long as they needed to. "Rose Rita can share Hilda's bedroom. That one belonged to the twins before we built the new part of the house, so there is an extra bed," Mrs. Weiss said. "And you, Mrs. Zimmermann, can sleep in our Trinka's old room. Trinka is our eldest, and she is married and moved away now. *Ach*, her husband is such a nice young man—"

One weird thing happened as Rose Rita was drying dishes. She noticed a calendar hanging on the wall behind the odd old sink with its hand-operated pump. The calendar said the year was 1828! Rose Rita leaned over for a closer look. All the days had been crossed off right up to February 23. "Is that the right date?" she asked Hilda.

"*Ja*, the twenty-third," Sarah said, pouring more hot water into the sink.

They went to bed not long after that. A cheery little fire burned in the small fireplace. The room smelled of oak and pine and peppermint, and it was comfortably warm. Hilda lent Rose Rita a fuzzy flannel nightgown, and Mrs. Weiss brought in a big stack of colorful quilts to keep her cozy through the night.

After Hilda blew out her candle, the only light in the room was the reddish flickering of the fire. Eventually even that burned down to just a glow. The girls talked a little in the darkness. Finally Rose Rita got up the nerve to ask, "Why did your father go to see a lawyer?"

Hilda said, "Because people have been saying Grampa Drexel is a *hexer*."

"A what?" Rose Rita asked. She knew the word, but she was interested in knowing more about Penn Dutch magic.

Hilda's voice sounded sleepy: "You know, a bad witch. All sorts of bad luck has happened this winter. Many people's cattle and chickens have sickened and died for no reason. There are even some people who have fallen ill. There have been dozens of mysterious fires in people's barns and houses. And even the schoolhouse. It burned to the ground two weeks ago."

"Sometimes I wish my school would burn down," Rose Rita confessed.

"Well," Hilda admitted, "I don't mind so much. But people say the weather is hexed too. One day it will be warm, almost like spring, and then we have a terrible blizzard."

"I don't understand," Rose Rita objected. "What has all this bad luck got to do with seeing a lawyer?"

For a long time Hilda did not answer. Then in a weepy voice she replied, "I told you. They say my grampa is a hex witch, that he has been doing black magic to cause all these awful things. People want us to leave our home."

Hilda was sobbing. Rose Rita felt terrible. She had not intended to hurt Hilda's feelings. "I'm sorry," she said.

Hilda snuffled. "Papa wanted to see if Lawyer Nuttenhaus could bring some legal action to make people stop talking about my grampa. But he said there was no law against gossip, and he told Papa to ignore what people are saying."

"Well, of course. I mean, your grampa Drexel isn't *really* a witch, is he?" Rose Rita asked.

"No, not a *hexer*. But I'm frightened, all the same. What if they chase us out of our house? What will become of us?"

Rose Rita bit her lip. She too was in trouble. She and Mrs. Zimmermann were lost in this strange world, with no way home. "That's all right," she said, trying to sound brave. "We'll find some way out of this mess."

"Thank you," Hilda whispered.

Rose Rita blinked in the dark. She had been talking to herself, but now she somehow felt that Hilda was right. To solve her own problem Rose Rita was going to have to help Hilda solve hers. She lay there in the dark trying to figure out some way of doing this. A long time later, warm and snug under all the quilts, Rose Rita at last drifted off into sleep. She had not even begun to find a way out of all the trouble.

CHAPTER FIVE

Hilda gently shook Rose Rita awake the next morning. "Time to get up," she said.

Rose Rita yawned and sat up in bed. The fire was out, and the room was frigid. A single candle gave a little dim yellow light. The window showed only a black square. "Good grief," Rose Rita muttered. "What time is it, anyway?"

"Already nearly five o'clock," Hilda said. "We'll be late to breakfast."

Rose Rita got up and dressed, but she still felt groggy and grumpy. She *never* got up at this hour. As far as she was concerned, five o'clock in the morning was still the middle of the night. But the household was up and bustling around, and Mrs. Zimmermann was among them. "The Weiss family is going to church this morning," she told Rose Rita. "Usually one of them must stay home with Grampa Drexel, because he hasn't been well lately. I told them they could all go to church, and the two of us will stay and keep Mr. Drexel company."

That was fine with Rose Rita. They had a second huge meal with the Weisses. Mrs. Weiss took a tray to Grampa Drexel, and the girls of the house all pitched in to tidy up after breakfast. Meanwhile, the men went out to see to the chores that had to be done on Sunday, the same as every other day: feeding the animals, milking the cows, and so on. The sun came up finally, bright and clear in a cold blue sky. All the Weisses bundled up and piled onto a big wagon. Mrs. Weiss stayed behind for a moment to give some fussy last-minute instructions: "Papa will be fine. He will probably keep to his bed today. Just look in from time to time to see if he needs anything." She told them where all the food was, when to check on Mr. Drexel, and about a hundred other details, until Mr. Weiss called for her, and then she hurried out.

"Well," Mrs. Zimmermann said as the wagon trundled away. "Alone at last, as they say in the movies. This is a pretty pickle we're in, Rose Rita!"

They sat at the table and enjoyed some coffee. "Mrs. Zimmermann, how are we ever gonna get home?" Rose Rita asked.

"I wish I knew. However, I believe I know *why* we are here. That is, I believe I know what we'll have to do before we can get a chance to return."

"What is it?"

Mrs. Zimmermann sighed. "In the first place here's a little bit of news for you. You've heard me talk about Granny Wetherbee, who taught me magic. Well, when she was young, Granny Wetherbee was Hilda Weiss—the little girl whose room you shared last night."

Rose Rita shook her head. "That's incredible. I don't understand it."

"I don't understand everything myself," Mrs. Zimmermann returned. "However, here is what I know: We have blundered into the Weiss family at a time of crisis. Their neighbors are all turning against them."

"I know," Rose Rita said. "Hilda told me that they all believe Mr. Drexel is a bad witch."

Mrs. Zimmermann nodded and sipped her coffee. "Yes, I remember Granny Wetherbee talking about that. Now I see that this experience is what turned her into a sour-tempered old woman. This is the year 1828. On April first of this year the family will be driven away from its home. And shortly after that, Grampa Drexel will die because of the journey."

Rose Rita swallowed hard. It was spooky and disturbing just to think about knowing when someone would die, and she felt a little pang of grief at the thought of Grampa Drexel's death. Of course, she wasn't well acquainted with him, but he had seemed a kindly old fellow at dinner, and she sensed that Hilda was greatly attached to him. "That's awful!" she said aloud.

"It is," agreed Mrs. Zimmermann. "You see, the Pennsylvania Dutch have a lot of odd superstitions. One of them is about April first. They see it as a very unlucky day, the worst in the year, sort of a Halloween and Walpurgis Night and Friday the Thirteenth all rolled into one. It's the day when evil witches and warlocks do their dirty deeds, and so the neighbors forced the family to move along before Grampa Drexel could cast any dire spells on that day. Unfortunately there was a late blizzard raging, and Grampa Drexel caught pneumonia and died."

"Can't we do anything?" Rose Rita asked.

"I hope so. You see, that is the reason we are here—or at least I *think* it is. Granny Wetherbee said nothing about a "great wrong" that happened in 1898—but this is surely a great wrong, and maybe we can help the family in 1828. If we can somehow save Mr. Drexel from his horrible fate, then Granny Wetherbee's ghost promises that I will get my powers back."

Rose Rita thought hard. "I don't see how we can do anything," she said. "I mean, to us all this is history. It already happened."

"I know," Mrs. Zimmermann said, sounding depressed. "I am not sure exactly what we've landed in. We may really be in the past, giving Grampa Drexel a second chance. Or maybe all this is a part of Granny Wetherbee's magic, some kind of grand, gorgeous hallucination or something. It may just be a way for her ghost to see what *would* have happened if things turned out differently. I know one thing, though: I want to go back to Bessie and get my mirror."

Rose Rita blinked. "So that's the mysterious package—the mirror!"

"What kind of mirror is that?" asked a mild, heavily accented voice. Rose Rita jumped in alarm. Standing in the doorway was Grampa Drexel, dressed in shirt, trousers, and slippers, and with a blanket around his shoulders like a shawl. "Forgive me," he said. "I did not mean to eavesdrop, but I heard part of your conversation." His bright-blue eyes twinkled as he gazed at Mrs. Zimmermann. "I thought I was not mistaken last night. Dear lady, you have more about you than meets the eye, *nicht*? What kind of mirror do you speak of? An *erdspiegel*, would it be?"

Mrs. Zimmermann gave Rose Rita a rueful grin. "I guess the jig is up. Here, Mr. Drexel, let me help you." She stood up and took Grampa Drexel's arm, steering him into a chair before the fireplace. "There," she said. "Well, to answer your questions, first, yes, I have a little bit of magic. Second, the mirror is enchanted, but the enchantment in it isn't mine. In fact, I don't know quite what it is. What did you call the mirror?"

"*Erdspiegel*," Grampa Drexel responded. "In English

an 'earth mirror.' People use them to find treasures and hidden things."

"I don't know about treasures, but my mirror sometimes shows me hidden things," Mrs. Zimmermann said. "I'm hoping it can show me a way to get myself and Rose Rita back to where we came from. We got here by some sort of magic, you see. Unfortunately, it isn't a kind that I can control."

Grampa Drexel nodded. "*Ja*, I sensed that you had something odd about you. Your magic, Mrs. Zimmermann, it is earth magic, or I am much mistaken. Good magic that is, healing magic. What we call *braucherei* here. It is the same kind as my own."

Rose Rita cleared her throat. "Uh—how much of our conversation did you hear?" she asked.

"Just a little, about the mirror," the old man answered.

Rose Rita gave Mrs. Zimmermann a look of relief. It would have been terrible if Grampa Drexel had overheard them talking about his death from pneumonia. Mrs. Zimmermann took the cue and said, "Mr. Drexel, why do people around here fear you?"

The old man shook his head sadly. "*Ach*, who knows? It is true that I have made cures for their illnesses over the years, but never, never have I made a hex or harmed anyone. But people spread terrible stories about bad magic they say I have done. I think Mr. Stoltzfuss is one of those who talk about me. He is a hard man, angry at the world, and for some reason he takes out his anger on me."

Rose Rita said, "Mrs. Zimmermann, maybe your mirror can answer questions for Mr. Drexel. You know, like 'Mirror, mirror on the wall.' "

Mrs. Zimmermann touched her chin with her forefinger. "That's a thought," she said slowly. "Anyway, maybe Mr. Drexel would know more about mirror magic than I ever did. That wasn't exactly my specialty."

"Go and get the *erdspiegel*," Mr. Drexel said. "I will be all right here. Take the small cart and the mule, Nebby. We will see what we will see."

Fortunately Mrs. Zimmermann had spent part of her girlhood on farms. She managed to hitch up the small green cart to Nebby, a dark-brown mule whose expression hinted that he would be happier doing anything else than pulling them. After Mr. Drexel insisted that he was perfectly fine, Mrs. Zimmermann agreed to let Rose Rita come along on the expedition.

It was a bright, cold day. They rumbled along to the foot of the hill, and there Mrs. Zimmermann reined Nebby in. "I don't trust myself to take us up there in this contraption," she said. "Rose Rita, how is your ankle today? Do you think you could climb up and get the mirror? I'd go myself, but this beast will head for home without someone at the reins who knows how to handle a mule."

"Sure," Rose Rita said. She got the car keys from Mrs. Zimmermann and climbed up the hill. Soon she was panting, the frigid air keen in her lungs. Her ankle hurt too, though it really was more stiff than sore. Still, she made good time, and before long she had dived into the thicket where poor Bessie waited. She unlocked the car and carefully took the wrapped mirror out of the backseat. Then she had to go downhill without dropping and breaking it. Going down took considerably longer than climbing up.

"I hope we can get home before the Weisses get back," she said as Mrs. Zimmermann turned the carriage.

"Don't worry about that," Mrs. Zimmermann said. "Church meetings were long affairs back in the 1820s. We probably have hours yet."

Nebby was in a better mood as soon as he realized they were heading home. He clopped along briskly. The snow was so bright that it hurt Rose Rita's eyes, and soon she was squinting. They arrived at the Weiss farm, and Rose Rita watched as Mrs. Zimmermann unhitched the carriage and took care of Nebby, rubbing him down and giving him a few extra handfuls of oats. Then they went back into the kitchen, where old Mr. Drexel sat in the rocking chair where they had left him, comfortably dozing. He woke up as the two of them came in.

Rose Rita added some wood to the fire, and for a few minutes she and Mrs. Zimmermann warmed themselves. Finally Mrs. Zimmermann carefully unwrapped the mirror. Mr. Drexel took it from her and looked at it critically. "*Ja*," he said at last. "This is an *erdspiegel*. The frame is mahogany, and the glass is backed with silver. If you hold the mirror just right, you can see some things written on the back plate. You see?"

Mrs. Zimmermann leaned close to examine the place Grampa Drexel indicated. "Really? Funny, but I never noticed any writing before. Of course, I never really had much reason to inspect the *back* of the mirror. Yes, now I can see the marks, but I can't read what they say."

Rose Rita looked on curiously. Grampa Drexel held the mirror facedown and tilted it, catching the firelight at various angles. She could barely make out a few scratchings on the back: a circle, a cross, and some marks that might have been letters. "It is not meant to be read easily. I would have to study the inscriptions to know what sort of spell this is," Grampa Drexel said. "But that can wait. Show me how you have used it, Mrs. Zimmermann, please."

Mrs. Zimmermann took it from him and set it up on the table, leaning it back against a tall, heavy earthenware jug. She braced the edge with the butter dish and the sugar bowl, so the mirror would not slip forward. Then she hesitated. After all, she had not really summoned the magic to begin with. It had sort of just happened. She was not at all certain that she could use the mirror in any constructive way now, and she was a bit uneasy about what might occur. But then, she thought, if she didn't at least try, they might never know. "All right," she said at last. "I'm going to look into the mirror and concentrate on a spirit that has appeared to me. It is the spirit of—well, of an old woman named Granny Wetherbee. I'm going to hope that she will appear and offer us advice on all our problems."

"Good," Grampa Drexel said. "I and Rose Rita, we will watch and be quiet."

Rose Rita moved over to stand beside Grampa Drexel. Now that they were actually going to begin this spooky stuff with the mirror, she felt a little afraid. From where she stood, she could see the mirror in front of Mrs. Zimmermann. Mrs. Zimmermann was almost in profile to Rose Rita, but she could see Mrs. Zimmermann's face reflected in the glass. For a long time Mrs. Zimmermann simply sat there, staring into the mirror. Then something began to happen. At first Rose Rita noticed little flickers of color at the edges of the mirror. These were weak flashes of rosy pink and more frequent ones of a pale, icy blue. Gradually these got stronger, until the whole surface of the mirror shimmered with changing colors. Then the skin on Rose Rita's neck and arms prickled. A face was forming in the mirror—and it was not Mrs. Zimmermann's face!

Rose Rita shivered. The face in the mirror was that of an old, old woman. She had a scowling brow and a mouth turned down from years of sorrow. The image was translucent. Behind it Rose Rita could faintly see the reflected face of Mrs. Zimmermann. The lips of the old woman moved, and a ghostly voice whispered from the mirror: "I hear you."

Rose Rita groped for Mr. Drexel's hand. He took her hand in his and gave her a reassuring squeeze. Mrs. Zimmermann was speaking now: "Tell us what to do."

"You know already," the ancient, whispery voice said. "Help the Weiss family. Then you may return, and you may find your lost magic again. Hurry! My time is short. Other powers are struggling to take the mirror from my control."

"But how can we help?" Mrs. Zimmermann said. "Make that clear to us—"

The image in the mirror faded, and for a moment Rose Rita could see only the reflection of Mrs. Zimmermann's face. Then, suddenly, two staring, cold eyes filled the whole mirror. They looked out with a glare of evil hatred that made Rose Rita shout aloud. Instantly the mirror flashed, and suddenly it went black. It reminded Rose Rita of the way the dark room had looked when she had first come in from the snow glare outside.

But this blackness was different. It emanated malice. "Don't look!" Mr. Drexel cried out. Rose Rita turned her head away.

She heard Mrs. Zimmermann gasp, and then she felt something like a silent explosion. "Help her," Grampa Drexel said. "It is safe now—help her, Rose Rita!"

Rose Rita ran to the table. Mrs. Zimmermann had slumped over, her forehead against the red-checked tablecloth in front of the mirror. The mirror, Rose Rita saw, was normal now, just an ordinary looking glass. Still, she turned it facedown. She shook her friend's shoulder. "Mrs. Zimmermann—Mrs. Zimmermann. Wake up. Oh, gosh, Mrs. Zimmermann, please wake up!"

Grampa Drexel had risen slowly and painfully. He stooped over Mrs. Zimmermann and touched her cheek. "She breathes normally. She will be all right, I think. The first image in the glass was good, but then some wicked force took over the mirror and tried to hurt her."

Mrs. Zimmermann's eyes fluttered open and she sat up, looking woozy. "My heavens," she said, "that was quite a shock!"

Rose Rita was almost crying. "Oh, I'm so glad you're all right," she said.

"Here now," Mrs. Zimmermann said with a puzzled glance. "Who are you? Should I know you?"

Rose Rita's heart jumped into her throat. "It's me, Mrs. Zimmermann! Rose Rita. Don't you remember me?"

"No. I'm afraid—" Mrs. Zimmermann touched her forehead with both hands. "I'm afraid I don't remember you. And for that matter," she said, "who am I? I can't seem to recall that, either."

CHAPTER SIX

Mrs. Zimmermann had completely lost her memory. She could not recall Rose Rita, Grampa Drexel, or even her own name. Rose Rita's heart sank at her friend's anxious, bewildered look. Mr. Drexel put his hand on her shoulder and said, "Get her into bed, please. I will try my herbs and remedies. Perhaps I can help her."

Rose Rita led Mrs. Zimmermann into the room where she had slept the night before. Mrs. Zimmermann seemed to feel that this strange girl was taking good care of her, and she went along obediently enough. Rose Rita helped her get undressed and into her borrowed night-gown. She had just snuggled into the bed when Grampa Drexel tapped softly at the door. Rose Rita let him in.

He carried a little black wooden box in his hands, which he set gently on the nightstand beside the bed. Mrs. Zimmermann stared at him with wide, frightened eyes. In a kind voice Grampa Drexel said, "Open the curtains, please, Miss Rose Rita. I need a little more light."

Rose Rita parted the curtains. The bright morning light spilled into the room as Grampa Drexel stooped over the bed. He touched Mrs. Zimmermann's forehead and murmured strange words. She blinked her eyes, and gradually the anxiety left them. Her eyelids fluttered and seemed to grow heavy. Mr. Drexel whispered to Rose Rita, "A glass of water, *bitte*."

Rose Rita hurried to the kitchen and found a glass. She worked the hand pump until the glass was full. When she returned and handed it to Grampa Drexel, he nodded gravely and murmured, "*Danke.*" He took a small brown vial from his box and poured about a teaspoon of thick green liquid into the water. Rose Rita wrinkled her nose as a pungent, stinging smell filled the air, a little like peppermint and a little like rubbing alcohol. Grampa Drexel swirled the glass until the water turned a pale-green tint, and then he helped Mrs. Zimmermann into a half-sitting position. She made a face at the first sip, but with Grampa Drexel's encouragement she got the whole glassful down. "Now I think you must sleep a bit," Grampa Drexel said.

Rose Rita waited anxiously at the foot of the bed. She knew something about amnesia, which is a loss of memory. Her father listened to lots of radio shows, like *Suspense* and *The Shadow* and *Inner Sanctum*, and people were always getting amnesia on them. Usually they got it by being whacked on the head, and sometimes they had to be hit hard again before they could remember who they were. Quite often when they regained their memory, they realized that they were murderers or spies, or that their best friend, husband, or wife was a murderer or spy.

As Rose Rita went through all she knew about amnesia, Mrs. Zimmermann's eyelids gradually closed, and she sighed. Soon she was sleeping peacefully. Grampa Drexel felt her pulse, nodded, and repacked his little box of medicines. "Good, good," he whispered. "She will sleep now, and perhaps when she wakes, she will be better, *nicht*? The shock will wear off, I believe. I think the curtains you may close now."

Rose Rita drew the curtains, and as she did so, she saw a small dark shape moving against the snow a long way off. It was the wagon! The Weiss family was returning from church! She hurried to the door, where Grampa Drexel stood, and told him that the family was coming back. "We have to hide the mirror," she finished.

"*Ja*," Grampa Drexel said. "That is a good thought. You are in the twins' old room. Take the mirror and hide it between the head of your bed and the wall. Wrap it up again, and turn it so the glass is against the wall. That way, I think it will be safe."

Rose Rita ran to the kitchen. In a way she hated even to touch the mirror, because she had sensed a horrible wave of evil pouring from it. It seemed to be just a mirror again, though, so she clumsily rewrapped it in the brown paper and rushed to the little room. She had to tug the bed away from the wall, but once she had done so, the mirror slipped right into place. It was hardly noticeable at all.

She expected to hear the family on the doorstep at any moment, but they had been very far away when she had noticed them. They had not even turned at Cottage Rock, and Rose Rita had plenty of time to get back to the kitchen. Grampa Drexel was sitting in his rocking chair there. He nodded as Rose Rita came in. "I think we shall say that your aunt had a little spell of dizziness," he told her. "They will think it was because she was out in the cold so long yesterday. I will treat her and try to bring her memory back."

"Can you do that?" Rose Rita asked, feeling lonely and sad and desperate.

Grampa Drexel smiled wearily. "Well, I can only try. But do not worry so much, Rose Rita. Someone used the mirror to do a wicked thing to Mrs. Zimmermann. But then, wicked things may be undone. You should remember, Miss Rose Rita, that good is stronger than wickedness. *Ja*, I do think Mrs. Zimmermann will get better—in time."

In time. Although Grampa Drexel did not know it,

he had only a little time left himself—if what Mrs. Zimmermann had told Rose Rita about April 1 was correct. What if he didn't have time to help Mrs. Zimmermann? What if she *never* regained her memory? It seemed to Rose Rita that things just went from bad to worse in this strange time and place.

At that moment the wagon rattled into the yard, and a few minutes after that the family came spilling in. Mrs. Weiss was very solicitous about Mrs. Zimmermann's health. She tutted and clucked and shook her head sympathetically as Grampa Drexel explained. Of course, she said, Mrs. Zimmermann and Rose Rita would stay with the family just as long as they needed to. The other children trailed in, all of them quiet and all looking miserable. Hilda's eyes were very red, as if she had been crying bitterly. Rebecca and Sarah, the twins, looked just as upset. The older boys' mouths were set in grim lines, and they hardly spoke. Shy, frightened-looking Heinrich seemed even more jumpy than ever.

As soon as she could, Rose Rita followed Hilda to the room they shared. The air felt chilly. Before church Mr. Weiss had built a small fire, but it had burned low. Rose Rita put some wood on the glowing embers, and soon cheerful yellow flames leaped with a lively crackling and hissing. Hilda changed from her Sunday dress into an everyday one and sat on her bed, staring at the floor.

Rose Rita sat on her own bed and asked Hilda,

"What's wrong? Why is everybody so gloomy?"

Hilda began to sniffle. "It was awful at meeting," she said. "Everybody in church just turned and glared at us when we came in. And the Hockendorf family got up and moved when Mama and the girls and I sat in the same pew. They all h-hate us." Hilda covered her face with her hands and began to cry.

Rose Rita went to sit on the bed beside Hilda. She put her arm around the other girl's shoulder. "It can't be all that bad," she said. "I don't think the people really *hate* you."

"They d-do," Hilda wailed. "They all th-think that Grampa is an evil wizard, and he's not. His m-magic is all good—" She broke off. In a small, miserable voice, she said, "I wasn't supposed to tell anyone about that."

"About your grampa's having magic?" Rose Rita asked. She bit her lip. Ordinarily she kept pretty quiet about magic and enchantments, because she knew very well that if you talked about things like that, most people figured you had a screw loose. But this was not an ordinary time. "Listen," she said at last. "I'm not supposed to say anything about this, either, but Mrs.— I mean, my aunt knows magic too."

Hilda was gasping a little. "Really?" she asked.

"Oh, sure," Rose Rita said. "She can pull matches right out of the air, and she can—"

"Pull what?" Hilda asked.

"Matches," Rose Rita said. "She uses them to light

her cigars. Only she's out of cigars, so she hasn't done it lately, and—"

"What are *matches*?" Hilda asked, sounding really puzzled.

Rose Rita blinked. She had not stopped to think that matches were something that had once been invented. It suddenly occurred to her that maybe matches did not even exist in 1828. "Uh, never mind," Rose Rita said. "But anyway, she used to have this wonderful umbrella with a purple crystal globe in the handle, and it glowed and gave her power—"

Hilda gave her a long, thoughtful look with eyes bleary from crying. After a moment she got off the bed and went to the little chest of drawers at its foot. "Promise you won't tell anyone about this?" she said. Her manner was mysterious and secretive.

Rose Rita nodded. "I promise," she said, feeling tingly and goose bumpy.

Hilda opened a drawer and took out a square box about the size of a building block. She opened it and took from inside it a sphere of clear crystal, no larger than a golf ball. "Watch," she said. She cupped the ball in her hands and bent her head over it. Her lips moved.

Rose Rita gasped. The crystal began to glow a soft rose color, very beautiful and very delicate. Hilda looked up and smiled for the first time. "Grampa Drexel awakened my magic," she whispered. "Only it's not very strong. I can't *do* anything except make the crystal light up. But he says my power will grow. One day I'll be able to cure people of sickness and help them find lost things and take hexes off them. I guess Mrs. Zimmermann has the same kind of magic."

"I guess so," Rose Rita said. She watched Hilda carefully replace the crystal, now dark again. She was thinking about how she might steal it, or at least borrow it. It was a great deal like the crystal that Mrs. Zimmermann had once owned, and Rose Rita thought it might help her friend find her magic power again. But when Hilda shut the drawer and gave her a weak smile, Rose Rita felt her resolve weakening.

"I guess we're best friends now," Hilda said shyly. "Because I haven't told any of my other friends about my magic."

Oh, great, Rose Rita thought. I sure can't steal that globe now! After a while Hilda went to do some of her chores, and Rose Rita wandered around the house feeling miserable and lonely. She borrowed a coat from Hilda and went out to look at the horses. Rose Rita was a town girl, but like a lot of girls her age she loved to read about horses. She went into the stables and saw Nicklaus, the big chestnut that had pulled the carriage, and a dappled gray mare, and a black one, and the mule, Nebby, down at the end, like a crabby neighbor. They all whickered softly in the dim, cold stable, their breath curling out in white plumes. Rose Rita heard another sound, a whimpering human sound. She decided that it came from overhead, and soon she found a ladder leading up to the hayloft.

She climbed up quietly. At the top she peeked into the loft. Heinrich, the youngest boy, had thrown himself onto the hay, and he was sniffling. "Hi," Rose Rita said. "What's the matter?"

Heinrich yelped and jumped to his feet. Then he turned his back. "Go away," he said, his voice trembling.

"Well, I just wanted to see if I could help," Rose Rita said.

Heinrich shook his head. "Nobody can help," he said. "Old Mr. Stoltzfuss wants to chase us away. And everyone is on his side."

Rose Rita went on up into the loft. It was warmer than the stables down below, and she sat on the crackly, sweet-smelling straw. "Tell me about Mr. Stoltzfuss," she demanded.

He made an angry face. "He is a devil," Heinrich said. "He tells everybody that my grampa causes the bad weather and the illnesses. He says the Weiss family must be driven out of town, and then everybody will be all better. He tells lies."

"Well, I'm sure that not everyone believes him."

"They do! They do!" Heinrich said. "And they will run us away from the farm. Papa knows they will. If only—" He broke off and turned away.

"If only what?" Rose Rita asked.

"You would laugh at me, like my brothers," Heinrich muttered.

Rose Rita sighed. This seemed to be her day for discovering the Weiss family secrets! "No, I won't," she said. "I promise."

Heinrich gave her a long, uncertain look. Finally he came over and sat next to her in the hay. "I will tell you," he said. "You are English—do you know what *fraktur* writing is?"

"Fractured writing?" Rose Rita asked. "I fractured my ankle, but—"

"*Nein, nein*," Heinrich said. "*Fraktur* writing. It is—I don't know how to say it, it is pretty writing, done by hand, and colored. Like a needlepoint the girls make."

"Oh," Rose Rita said. "You mean the kind of handwriting in mottos? I noticed that your family has some framed."

"*Ja*," Heinrich said. "The writing in the mottos, as you say. But one of them is different." He leaned close and whispered, "Have you ever heard of the Donniker treasure?"

Rose Rita shook her head.

"Well, back in the days of General Washington, the town of Donniker had a chest of gold and silver that they had collected to help the American army. Only the British found out about it, and they sent Hessian soldiers to steal the treasure. Three men from Donniker were supposed to take the treasure and get it to General Washington or hide it before the British could get their hands on it. And one of them was the first Heinrich Weiss, my grandpapa!"

Rose Rita blinked. Now that she thought about it, the Revolution had happened only about fifty-two years ago for the Weiss family. Still, talking to someone whose grandfather had fought with General Washington was unsettling. "What happened?" she asked.

"The Hessian soldiers tracked down my grandpapa and his friends and attacked them. They had to run away through the woods, carrying the heavy chest full of money. After days of being chased, they came to the valley here. They buried the treasure to keep it safe, and they went in separate directions. The British caught the other two men and hanged them. My grandpapa was captured too, but he played dumb. He pretended not to speak any English. They put him in jail for years. When he got out, he was too sick to come back to the valley. But while he was still in prison, he wrote down where the treasure was, in *fraktur* writing. He did it in English, which is not usual. He gave the writing to my grandmama. She came to this valley with the family, and she and her sons bought this farm. The treasure is supposed to be buried somewhere on it. If we could find that—well, if we could, then it wouldn't matter what lies old Mr. Stoltzfuss told. We could move anywhere we pleased!"

"Why doesn't your father dig the treasure up, then?" Rose Rita asked.

Heinrich shook his head. "No one can figure out the writing," he confessed. "It is like a riddle. People have looked and looked, but no one has found it."

Rose Rita was intrigued. She enjoyed mysteries and puzzles of all sorts, and she was good at solving them. "I'll bet *I* could figure it out," she said.

Heinrich looked doubtful. "But my papa gave up looking for it years and years ago. My uncle Benjamin was the oldest, and he searched for it for years before he died. Then my uncle George searched for it until he moved to Harrisburg. And my papa, the youngest, looked for it for years until he gave up. He thinks that maybe my grandpapa wasn't right in the head when he wrote the riddle."

"Let me try," Rose Rita said with confidence. "I'll bet I can figure out the secret. Anyway, it won't hurt to try, will it? And if we succeed, you can just forget about mean old Mr. Stoltzfuss."

Heinrich brightened a bit at that. "*Ja*, that is true," he said. "All right. I will have to try to sneak the *fraktur* out of the big Bible without anyone knowing. I'll tell you when I have got it, and you can look at it."

"Fine," Rose Rita said. "Now I don't know about you, but I'm freezing. I'm going inside to warm up."

The gloom that gripped the Weiss family did not loosen its hold that evening. Supper was a quiet affair.

Rose Rita took Mrs. Zimmermann's meal to her on a tray, and Mrs. Zimmermann thanked her absentmindedly. Once she said suddenly, "Whatever happened to Bessie?" But when Rose Rita tried to answer, Mrs. Zimmermann looked blank and murmured, "I had a car named Bessie?"

Rose Rita realized that she had a big problem on her hands. Mrs. Zimmermann could not remember much, but she knew all about automobiles and television and radio. Rose Rita would have to stick close by her friend while she recovered. She could just imagine what would happen if Mrs. Zimmermann began asking to hear a Detroit Tiger game on the radio or saying that she would like to see the new John Wayne western at the Bijou. The Weisses would probably lock her up in a loony bin!

That night Rose Rita fell asleep very early. Some time later she woke up because of a noise. She lay in bed breathing quietly for a few moments, and then she heard it again: a dog barking furiously. Then suddenly it stopped. Not like an ordinary dog would stop, with a few last angry yelps, but like a record when the needle is quickly lifted. Rose Rita put her glasses on and slipped out of bed. The floor was cold beneath her bare feet, and despite the flannel nightgown she wore, she shivered.

She could see nothing from the window in the room, so she tiptoed into the hall and went to a window that looked out the front of the house. The moonlight made the snow pearly. She knelt on the floor, rested her forehead against the cold glass, and stared out. She saw the dog after a moment. It was a big dark mongrel, but it looked more like a statue than a real dog: It stood absolutely still, with its back to the house.

Then something moved, something dark against the snow, and Rose Rita saw a flash of light. She blinked. The dark shape was a man, bundled up and hunched over. He held something in his hand. In fact he held two somethings: One was small and round, and the other was large and square. The large, square thing was a mirror, she saw. The moon's reflection in it had been the flash of light. The man held the large mirror in his left hand and tilted it. Meanwhile, he seemed to be looking at the reflection in the large mirror through the small object, another mirror. He turned slowly. The dog never moved.

Rose Rita could not figure out what was going on. She could not see very well, either, because frost had feathered the windowpane. She quietly raised the window sash. A blast of icy air swept in, and when she had the window open about six inches, she knelt again and peeked out through the opening. Yes, it was a tall, heavily wrapped man, and yes, he did indeed hold two mirrors. He turned in a slow circle, and Rose Rita heard a thin, high voice chanting some half-musical incantation. The window suddenly slipped down and shut with a snap.

Rose Rita gasped. The figure had turned to stare up at the house, and the man's eyes glowed. They were filled with a wicked hatred. She had seen them before: They were the eyes that had stared out of Mrs. Zimmermann's mirror!

The man held the small round mirror high above his head, and again light flashed out of it. The light blinded Rose Rita for a moment. She leaped to her feet, pulled her glasses off, and rubbed her eyes. Suddenly she felt very cold. Tears ran from her eyes, and when she blinked them away, she saw to her astonishment that she was no longer standing in the hallway. She was outdoors, and under her bare feet was the cold, snowy ground. It was a dark night, with just a little hint of moonlight. Rose Rita put her glasses back on and could see a little better. All around her glimmered white-marble oblongs and ovals and squares. Rose Rita's skin crawled. She was standing in a graveyard!

She turned helplessly this way and that, but the rows of tombstones stretched on in every direction. She wanted to run, but the grave markers were so thick, they threatened to trip her. She tried to walk between them. She stepped on a low mound, a snow-covered grave, and to her shock she heard a muffled voice below her feet: "Who is that up there? I want company!"

With horror she felt the earth heave beneath her, as if something were burrowing up toward her like a monstrous mole. She ran, her weak ankle stabbing with pain.

Mocking laughter echoed all around her. She looked over her shoulder. The graves were all erupting! Bony arms thrust upward everywhere, lashing around and scrabbling. Other graves were wide open, and skeletons clad in rotting clothes were hoisting themselves out of the ground, turning their horrible dirt-caked grins in her direction. The closest ones reached for her legs and tried to trip her.

The black mongrel dog came running behind her, snarling, its eyes glowing a fiery red. Liquid fire drooled from its black lips. Rose Rita tripped over a stone and stumbled. She landed sprawling facedown, her nose crunching into the stinging snow. Instantly cold, icy, skeletal fingers closed over her arms and legs, and the awful smell of decay filled her nose. A gritty, dirt-clogged, cackling laugh burst from the skeletons. The dog wailed and howled close by. The skeletons picked her up, her glasses fell off, and Rose Rita felt herself being tossed through the air. She saw that she was being thrown into a gaping fresh grave. Moonlight touched the marker at its head. The words "HERE LIES A SPY" were carved into it. It was the last thing that Rose Rita saw before she passed out.

She woke shivering some time after that. She was lying flat on her back. She threw her arms upward, expecting to touch the closed lid of a coffin, but there was nothing above her. For a moment she wondered who she was and where she was, and then it all came flooding back. The window was above her, and she lay on the floor of the Weiss family's upstairs hallway. Her glasses were still perched on her nose. The graveyard had been a horrible nightmare or hallucination. Rose Rita raised herself stiffly and stared out the window. The dog, the man, and the mirrors were all gone. Spookiest of all, the snow lay smooth and unmarked. Not even a footprint showed that something strange and eerie had been going on out there.

CHAPTER SEVEN

A whole week went by, during which, to Rose Rita's relief, Mrs. Zimmermann slowly got better. By Wednesday she knew who she was, and she usually recognized Rose Rita. But she still had lingering problems. Mrs. Zimmermann could not seem to keep clear in her head where she and Rose Rita were or what had happened to them. Sometimes she thought she was back home, and she would ask Rose Rita to turn on the radio, or she would suggest inviting Jonathan and Lewis over for supper. At other times she relived her younger days. She would talk about her tour through France in 1912 and 1913 as if she had just returned, or she would worry about the classes she thought she was still taking at the

University of Göttingen. But there were also flashes when she was quite sharp about everything. Finally she snapped out of her confusion on the first Monday in March.

"I've been out of my head, haven't I? Really 'round the bend?" Mrs. Zimmermann asked Rose Rita that morning. Mrs. Zimmermann was propped up with pillows, a breakfast tray on her lap, and Rose Rita was sitting on the foot of the bed. Mrs. Zimmermann shook her head, looking worried. "I can't seem to remember very much after looking into the mirror. What happened?"

Rose Rita was overjoyed to find Mrs. Zimmermann so well. She hurriedly told her friend about everything that she had seen. Mrs. Zimmermann listened, a frown deepening on her face. At last she said, "I never expected that mirror to turn on me. Well, I'm lucky that I am a witch. I may not have all my magic, but there's enough left to protect me—at least a little."

Rose Rita blinked. "Protect you? But the mirror knocked you loopy! You didn't know who I was, or who you were, or anything."

Mrs. Zimmermann smiled. "Yes, and I got off light at being knocked loopy, as you call it. Why, I expect that sorcerous attack would have made anyone but a witch a blithering moron for life! It was horrible, malevolent magic at its worst, and there was a strong power behind it. Fortunately, when black magic assaults white magic, the white magic sort of automatically defends itself. I didn't have time to cast a spell, but my magic tried its best to take care of me." She sighed. Improved though she was, Mrs. Zimmermann still looked terrible. Her face was alarmingly thin, her hands trembled with weakness, and her eyes still had not regained their sparkle. "Well," she said at last, "I suppose there's no help for it. You'll have to bring me the mirror again, and I'll try to get in touch with Granny Wetherbee's ghost—"

Rose Rita jumped up. "Gosh, no, Mrs. Zimmermann! I mean, what if it happened again? This time your magic might not be able to save you."

"Now, don't talk nonsense," Mrs. Zimmermann said, gruffly. "We are in a terrible situation. You're due home in a day or two, and here we are stuck in the past. I've got to try to remedy things."

Rose Rita could be extremely stubborn. She put her foot down. "I won't bring you the stupid mirror, so you can't try to use it. Remember what Granny Wetherbee's ghost told you? We have to help Grampa Drexel, and then we can go home again. Well, Heinrich and I are going to help Grampa Drexel, so there."

"Good heavens, don't be so touchy," Mrs. Zimmermann said. "I can see that I've been out of it too long. All right, Miss Rose Rita Pottinger! Tell me what you're up to. I warn you, if it's dangerous, I won't stand for it. You may keep me from risking my scrawny old neck with the mirror, but I can keep you from running off and pulling some fool stunt that might get you killed!"

"It isn't a stunt," Rose Rita said, in a grouchy voice. "Heinrich—do you remember which one he is?"

Mrs. Zimmermann nodded. "The youngest Weiss boy. The one who looks like a skinned rabbit."

"He does not!" Rose Rita said. "And if you won't be nice, I won't even tell you."

Mrs. Zimmermann laughed. "We've been through too much together to quarrel," she said. "Peace! All right, what are you and Heinrich up to?"

Rose Rita licked her lips. She was not sure how much Mrs. Zimmermann remembered about the problems of the Weisses. "Well, the family is going to have to move because somebody is spreading awful stories about Grampa Drexel. Heinrich and I are going to find out what's behind the stories. You told the Weisses that we were looking for relatives. Heinrich is going to drive me to the farms in the neighborhood so I can ask about our Zimmermann cousins. And while I'm there, I'll snoop around and find out why anyone would want to spread the tales about Grampa Drexel's being a hex witch."

"Does Heinrich have time to do that?" Mrs. Zimmermann asked. She knew how hard frontier farm families had to work.

"Oh, sure," Rose Rita said. "The school burned down last month, and everyone sort of decided not to try to get it going again until springtime. So he doesn't have to go to school right now. And the Weiss family can spare him to drive me around, because he's the youngest and doesn't do too much. They couldn't let one of the older boys go, but Heinrich is—what is that word?"

"Expendable," Mrs. Zimmermann said dryly. "Is that all?"

"Well, sort of." Rose Rita paused. Should she tell Mrs. Zimmermann about the riddle done in *fraktur* writing? Heinrich had tried several times to get it, but the big Bible was in his parents' bedroom, and he had never managed to sneak it out. "There's something else," Rose Rita said at last, "but it may not help. I'll tell you more about that later on."

And there the matter rested. Later that day Heinrich hitched the mule, Nebby, up to the little green cart, and the two of them set out to visit some of the neighboring farms. It was a blustery day, warmer than it had been, with low, white clouds speeding overhead and their shadows racing across the ground. The snow had melted a little, but there was still plenty of it on the shady sides of the hills.

The first farm they came to was the next one down the road. It was the Pilcher place. Rose Rita talked to Mrs. Pilcher, a chubby, jolly-looking woman. Mrs. Pilcher did not know of any Zimmermanns in the valley, naturally enough, but she had heard the stories about Grampa Drexel. She obviously felt sorry for the Weiss family. "Such a terrible thing," she said, shaking her head. "Awful stories they tell, but I don't believe half of them." But Mrs. Pilcher did not help a lot when Rose Rita tried to find who *they* were, or exactly what stories *they* told. The farm woman merely shook her head. "Oh, they say that all the terrible weather is because of a hex, and all the animals that have died, and all the people sick this winter. It's a worry, I can tell you!"

Heinrich and Rose Rita visited five other farms. Rose Rita soon noticed a pattern. The farther they got from the Weiss house, the more prejudiced the people became. Finally Heinrich would let Rose Rita climb off the wagon out of sight of the next farm house, and she would walk along the road alone. If the farmers or their families even caught sight of the Weiss mule and carriage, they refused to answer the door. Rose Rita did run into a gossipy old woman at the next-to-last place, a Mrs. Kleinwald. She mumbled darkly about the "wizard Drexel" and said that Mr. Stoltzfuss had talked to her son about all the wickedness that Grampa Drexel had done.

So later, when Heinrich and Rose Rita reached a crossroads, Rose Rita asked, "Which way does that Mr. Stoltzfuss live? We oughta try him next."

Heinrich looked at her as if she had suggested they set fire to each other. "Are you crazy in the head?" he squeaked. "He's a mean one, Mr. Stoltzfuss. He don't even come to church much, but he's always the first to say someone else is doing the devil's work."

"Well," Rose Rita said reasonably, "he's the one to see, then. Where does he live?"

Heinrich shook his head. "His farm is that way," he said, nodding toward the road that led away to the right. "But I don't think it's good to call on him."

"How far is it?"

Heinrich shrugged miserably. "Not very far. But he is a mean one, Mr. Stoltzfuss."

Rose Rita badgered Heinrich until the boy turned the mule onto the road leading to the Stoltzfuss farm. On the way he told her that Mr. Stoltzfuss was a widower who lived all alone. His farm had once been larger, but he had sold off little pieces of it over the years. Now it was just a small place. The wagon creaked up a hill, and Heinrich slowed Nebby's pace. "There," he said, pointing to a small, gambrel-roofed house and a large, dilapidated barn. "That is Mr. Stoltzfuss's farm. I don't want to go any closer."

"Then you wait here," Rose Rita said, and she hopped down from the carriage. By this time the afternoon sun had warmed things up quite a bit. The road was sloppy and muddy, and rivulets of water ran from the melting banks of snow. Rose Rita walked carefully, but her sneakers soon got soaking wet. She didn't much like the look of Mr. Stoltzfuss's house as she approached it. It was much smaller than the Weiss home. It had two stories, but it was all in one block, not a central house with two wings, like the Weiss place. And about half the windows had been broken. Boards were nailed over them. The remaining windows looked dark and dingy. The whole house was a weathered gray. It had not been painted in a long time.

Rose Rita walked right up to the front door and knocked. No one answered her second knock, or her third. Thinking that maybe Mr. Stoltzfuss was in the barn, she headed around to the back of the house. As she passed a window, she could not resist peeking in. What she saw made her stop and stare. She tiptoed up to the window and shaded her eyes with her hands.

She was looking into a weird room. The walls were painted with hex signs, dozens of them. A long black table in the center of the room and a black trunk were the only furniture she could see. Lying on the table was a sword, and beside it was an incense burner, a brass contraption that looked like a little fireplace and chimney. Rose Rita was looking past a stack of books that had been carelessly placed on the windowsill. She squinted through the dirty glass. She could see the front cover of one of the books, and the spine of a second. The first book was called *The Sixth and Seventh Books of Moses*, and the second was *The Long-Lost Friend.*

Just then Rose Rita heard a sound. She moved away from the window just in time. A tall, skinny man dressed in a wide-brimmed black hat and a long black coat came out of the barn and stopped suddenly when he saw her. Rose Rita recognized him as the same old man who had cursed at Mr. Weiss that day Mr. Weiss had given her and Mrs. Zimmermann the ride. He walked quickly toward her and growled, "Why are you trespassing?" His voice was harsh and high-pitched, like a fingernail scraping a blackboard.

"Uh, I—I'm looking for some relatives," Rose Rita stammered. "My aunt and I are trying to—"

"Lies!" Mr. Stoltzfuss snarled. "I can tell a liar when I see one!"

Rose Rita was scared, but she was angry too. "Don't call me a liar," she said. "I'm not the one who goes spreading lies about poor old Mr. Drexel!"

The mean eyes narrowed and grew crafty. "*Ach*, you know that hellhound? Then you are probably in league with him! Get off my land!" Something about the way he glared at Rose Rita made her shiver. Without a word she turned and ran back around to the front of the house. She heard the rumble of the carriage. Heinrich stopped just in front of the house, and Rose Rita clambered aboard. Then Heinrich flicked Nebby with the thin whip, and the mule clattered away.

Rose Rita looked back. The tall, thin Mr. Stoltzfuss stood beside his house, his hands clenched at his sides. "So!" he shouted after them. "Another little spy! I'll take care of you!"

The rest of his threat faded in the racket of the mule and wagon. Poor Nebby was about as frightened as Rose Rita had been, and for the first time that day he actually made good speed. Heinrich had some trouble controlling him. Rose Rita looked back. Stoltzfuss stood in the center of the road behind them. He was waving his arms in a strange way, and all of a sudden Rose Rita felt very sleepy and dull and dreamy. When Heinrich spoke, his voice sounded thin and faint, as if it came from far away: "We can go on to the next crossroads and then come back to the high road not far from our farm."

"Let's do that," Rose Rita said. She hated to admit how scared she had been.

They got back to the farm not long before sunset. Rose Rita found Grampa Drexel sitting beside Mrs. Zimmermann's bed, giving her some more of the smelly green tonic. "Your aunt is better today," he said as Rose Rita came in.

That was true, but Mrs. Zimmermann had a long way to go. She had slipped back into confusion earlier in the day, Grampa Drexel said. Now she was better again, but she still was so drawn and haggard that her appearance worried Rose Rita. The drink that Grampa Drexel had prepared did its work, and soon Mrs. Zimmermann was sleeping. Rose Rita told Grampa Drexel about the day's expedition, and about what had happened. When she was about to describe the books she had seen through Mr. Stoltzfuss's window, she paused. For some reason she could not bring herself to mention them. It did not seem important to her, and so she said nothing about the hex signs or the black table or the stack of suspicious books.

Grampa Drexel shook his head. "*Ach*, I do not know why Adolphus Stoltzfuss should such a hard man be. Once his father fought for the British. Maybe he is still regretting the Revolution, *nicht?*" Grampa Drexel rose on shaky legs. He trembled with exhaustion as he reached for his box of herbs and medicines.

Rose Rita said, "I'll help you with that." She carried the box back to Grampa Drexel's room. He asked her to put it on a shelf beside his bed. As she did so, Rose Rita paused. She stared hard at some books on the shelf and reached out to touch their spines. She read the titles: *The Sixth and Seventh Books of Moses* and *The Long-Lost Friend.* They were just like two of the books she had seen through Mr. Stoltzfuss's window! Rose Rita turned to tell Grampa Drexel about Mr. Stoltzfuss's books. Her tongue would not work! She fought to speak, but she could not say a word! Then she remembered the strange gestures she had seen Stoltzfuss make as she and Heinrich drove away. Had he put some spell of silence on her? Was Adolphus Stoltzfuss the hexer?

As soon as the thought came to her, Rose Rita felt sleepy and confused. A moment later she could not quite remember what she had been thinking about. But she still had a finger against the spine of *The Long-Lost Friend.* Finally she managed to ask a question: "Grampa Drexel, what kind of books are these?"

Grampa Drexel had sunk into an armchair. From its depths he looked at her gravely. "Books of magic these are. Some have evil spells in them too. But I have them only so I will know how to counteract the bad spells. I believe in magic that is used for good purposes only, never for evil." He leaned forward in his chair, and his voice grew urgent: "Let me warn you about such books, Miss Rose Rita. Some of them have powerful hexes. Stories there are of one book that is full of spells to conjure up evil spirits. These spells do not need to be spoken aloud. They work if someone only reads them silently. Worse, if an innocent victim begins to read these spells, he or she cannot stop. The words will trap the victim into finishing the spell. And once the spell is completed, then a terrible demon may show up with no control over its actions. The unlucky reader will be torn in pieces!"

Rose Rita shivered and swallowed hard. "Then how can *anyone* read the books?"

With a weary smile Grampa Drexel said, "*Ach*, there are ways. Counterspells of protection. And if a smart person finds himself trapped by one of the terrible spells, he can get out again if he takes every step backward.

But never find yourself in such a predicament, Miss Rose Rita! Leave such books to old fellows like me, who are too tough for demons to eat."

Rose Rita tried hard to remember what had first attracted her attention to the books. She vaguely remembered seeing books like them somewhere else, but she could no longer recall just where. She sighed. "Are all these books full of awful magic like that?"

Grampa Drexel tilted his head. "*The Long-Lost Friend* and the books of Moses? *Nein*, they are simply filled with remedies and good charms. Powwow books, some name them. I suppose it is possible an evil person might get an idea about how to do some wicked deeds from these books, but me they teach how to help others."

Rose Rita thought of how Grampa Drexel had been trying to help poor Mrs. Zimmermann. Although she was improving, Mrs. Zimmermann still seemed worn out and old. Rose Rita remembered how she had looked asleep. Her gray hair, never very tidy, straggled across the pillow, and her face was frail and weak. Rose Rita said, "Grampa Drexel, can I ask you for a big, big favor?"

"What, child?"

"Will you help Mrs. Zimmermann get her magic back? She is a good witch too, but she lost all her power trying to help a friend of mine." Rose Rita told Grampa Drexel about the horrible moment when Lewis had almost been lured to his death by a vengeful spirit, and how Mrs.

Zimmermann had put everything she had into saving him.

Grampa Drexel closed his eyes. After a long time he whispered, "*Ja*, it is a pity such courage and love should make Mrs. Zimmermann lose her magic. There may be a way. Come."

He led Rose Rita to a small room on the second floor of the house. It was a sort of attic, jumbled with old furniture, broken lanterns, and other odds and ends. Mr. Drexel searched until he found a wooden chest. He opened it, and from within he took a small crystal, just like the one that Hilda had shown her—except this one was dark.

"This is my last one," Grampa Drexel said. "When I was a young man, seven of these I made. Six of them I have given to those whose magic I have sensed and helped awaken. This one I have saved. I think I have saved it for your friend." He held the crystal out, and Rose Rita took it. It was cool, smooth, and heavy in her hand.

"What do I do with it?" she asked.

Grampa Drexel smiled. "Usually I notice the spark of magic in a young girl, and I prepare the crystal. Many years later I give it to her."

"Many *years*?" Rose Rita asked, appalled. She didn't know if Mrs. Zimmermann could hold out for very many years without her powers.

Grampa Drexel nodded. "Yes. It is earth magic. For

the crystal to gain full power, it must be buried in the earth for at least seven years. The longer it rests there, the more power it gains. And then when it is dug up again, it must be touched first by the one who will wield it. There is also a ceremony to perform when it is buried." He went on to explain that the crystal had to be named for the one it would serve. Then he had to pronounce a charm over it. Finally, it had to be buried in earth under a waxing crescent moon. "And that is some time off," he finished. "I believe the time will be right on the seventeeth of this month."

Rose Rita blinked. The seventeenth of March was just two weeks before April 1. If Granny Wetherbee had told the truth, Grampa Drexel himself was fated to fall fatally ill on April 1. Mrs. Zimmermann was not the only one who was running out of time.

CHAPTER EIGHT

A good deal of time went by before Heinrich finally had an opportunity to slip the sheet of *fraktur* writing out of its hiding place in the family Bible. In a household as large as that of the Weiss family, someone was almost always around to notice you slipping into someone else's room. Rose Rita nagged at Heinrich to hurry up, but the poor boy just couldn't find an opportunity, and days passed without his getting the prize.

Rose Rita spent four of them traveling around the valley to the various farms. She confirmed that the closer the farmers lived to the grouchy old Mr. Stoltzfuss, the more they seemed to hate Grampa Drexel. Other than that one single fact, there seemed little else to learn. Since Rose Rita really wasn't accomplishing very much, she stayed on the Weiss farm after that. Mrs. Zimmermann still wavered between being lucid and being slightly out of her head, and Rose Rita had to protect her against making any terrible mistakes, like asking Mrs. Weiss what she thought of President Truman. But then about the middle of March, Heinrich finally smuggled the mysterious paper out to the stables, and together he and Rose Rita inspected it.

The fabulous coded message disappointed Rose Rita. The paper was old and heavy, creamy brown and dusty smelling. The message was done in red, black, and green ink, in a fancy script with lots of flourishes and curliques, which made it hard to read. The same inks had been used to draw a complicated floral frame around the words. Rose Rita wasted some time in studying this, thinking that maybe the border was some kind of tricky chart.

She finally decided that it was just a bunch of flowers and vines, and the clues must be in the poem itself, not in the floral border around it. But the message was not a map, like in *Treasure Island*, or an obvious code, like in Edgar Allan Poe's story "The Gold Bug." Instead, with Heinrich's help Rose Rita read a rather poorly done poem:

To the Sons of Liberty, That They Mite
Discover the Welth of Freedom

Step ye sons of freedom smart;
Liv with liberty in your hart.
Paces the foe with heavy tred;
North, your countrymen are lying dead.
From Boston, from Concord, from Lexington,
Cottage and mansion send forth their sons.
Rock-hard the hart of the British soldier,
Then harder still are we, and bolder.
Line your rebelion with corage brave;
Great harts will live where our flag shall wave.
Tree and river shall hide our arms
And as ye hear war's loud alarms,
Mountain and hill, and valley so deep,
Dig like the foxx your den to keep.
For if we keep fayth, our people true,
Treasure of liberty must be our due.

This-Vers-Made-By-Heinrich-Weiss-MDCCLXXVIII
The-First-Shall-Find-Riches.

Well, Rose Rita thought, however pretty his handwriting might be, old Heinrich Weiss wasn't much of a speller. "Mite" and "welth" and "liv" indeed! But then, she reminded herself, he had been an immigrant from Germany and probably had learned English only with difficulty. "It doesn't *look* like a code," she told young Heinrich.

"But it mentions treasure," the boy said. "Right in the title is the word *wealth*. And after the poem is over, he says that the first to solve it will find the riches."

"MDCCLXXVIII," Rose Rita said. "I know those are Roman numerals, but I can't go that high. What is it, an amount of money?"

"No, it is the date," Heinrich said in a surprised voice. "It means 1778. That was the year my grandpapa died. My father was only two years old."

Rose Rita had to remind herself that Hermann Weiss was only fifty-two now, in 1828. She still could not get out of the habit of thinking the year was 1951. "Well," she said, "I suppose we ought to copy this. Then we can work on solving the puzzle and not have to worry about your folks noticing that the original is gone." Heinrich went into the house and brought out paper, ink, and a quill pen. Rose Rita had some difficulty with this—the tip kept wanting to spread out and drag a big blob of ink down the page—but Heinrich had a penknife and patiently shaped a new point for her several times. Finally she copied out the poem, terrible spelling and all, except that she did it in her normal handwriting. She made no attempt to copy the complex script of the original. Heinrich was able to smuggle the original back into the Bible without anyone being the wiser.

The reason that Heinrich could do this was not a comforting one. Grampa Drexel had gone on treating Mrs. Zimmermann with his herbs and medicines, but he was feeble himself. The strain of trying to help Mrs. Zimmermann was making him worse. Rose Rita helped

Hilda take care of him on the days when he was so ill that he could hardly stir from his bed. Mrs. Weiss, who fluttered all around the house (usually talking a mile a minute), sometimes had to feed her stepfather. It was while she was serving him meals that Heinrich slipped the paper in and out of Mr. and Mrs. Weiss's bedroom.

Rose Rita was very concerned about Mr. Drexel's health. Of course, he had promised to create a magic charm that would bring back Mrs. Zimmermann's witchy powers, but aside from that, Rose Rita had become fond of the old man. He was always gentle and understanding, and on the increasingly rare days when he was not feeling terribly ill, he had a great sense of humor. Inside he was more like one of the rowdy Weiss children than an old fellow. It hurt Rose Rita to see him lying in bed, pale and weak, with a tired, pained look on his face. Rose Rita knew that Hilda was very worried too.

One night as they lay in Hilda's room, with only the red embers of the fire giving any light, Hilda whispered to Rose Rita that she feared her grandfather was the victim of an evil curse.

Rose Rita was quiet for a long time. A couple of years earlier she would have told Hilda that evil curses and wicked witches were nonsense, that they didn't exist. But being a friend of Mrs. Zimmermann's and Jonathan Barnavelt's meant that Rose Rita had seen some pretty weird events. She knew that some people could indeed use magic, and she had discovered that evil people could use magic for wicked purposes. Now she said, "Is that what your grampa thinks, Hilda?"

"Yes," Hilda said in a weepy voice. "He thinks someone must have made a hex doll of him."

Rose Rita had heard a little about this. She knew that those who wanted to practice harmful magic sometimes made images of people they wished to injure. Mrs. Zimmermann had told her once that an evil witch might use a photograph of an enemy in a ceremony that harmed the picture and also harmed the victim. A voodoo doll was like that. It was a small wax effigy made by a witch doctor to resemble some living person. The witch doctor then stuck the doll full of pins. The victim was then supposed to suffer illness or excruciating pain in the same part of his or her body where the pins were stuck. She guessed that a hex doll was pretty much the same thing. "I bet I know who would do that," she said. "Old Stoltzfuss." Then a strange thing happened: Rose Rita's tongue seemed to stick in her mouth. She could say nothing more about Stoltzfuss. When she struggled to talk, her mind whirled, and in a moment she could not remember who she had been talking about.

"I don't know," Hilda said. For a long time she lay sobbing quietly.

Rose Rita tried to think of something that would cheer Hilda. The two girls had shared the room for about a month, and they had gradually come to be almost like sisters. Even Mrs. Weiss, with her talkative, fussy ways, tended to treat Rose Rita like just another member of the large family by this time. So Rose Rita knew the kinds of things that Hilda liked to talk about. After many minutes had passed, Rose Rita asked, "Will there be any frolics this spring?" She knew that the Penn Dutch called dances *frolics*, and she knew that Hilda eagerly looked forward to finally being old enough to go to one.

"Everything has been so bad this winter, I don't know," Hilda said. After a pause she added, "I hope there will be. My oldest sister, Trinka, told me all about them."

"Uh-huh," Rose Rita said. She had heard bits and pieces of this story before, because it was one that Mrs. Weiss like to tell over and over. She yawned. She was really sleepy, but she decided to try to stay awake long enough to be sure that Hilda's mind was off hexes and evil wizards and voodoo dolls. "Trinka met her husband at a frolic, didn't she?"

"Yes," Hilda said. Her voice was a little dreamy. Rose Rita got the idea that she was fond of her oldest sister's husband, a young man named Edgar Dienst. "She was seventeen. Edgar was visiting his uncle in the valley, and he came to the frolic with his cousins. Edgar was twenty then. When Trinka saw him, she thought he was the most handsome man in the world, and when Edgar saw her, he told his cousins that this was the girl he wanted to marry. And sure enough, one year later, they did get married. I wore the prettiest dress." Hilda sighed in contentment. She thought her sister's courtship was just like a fairy tale. She asked Rose Rita, "Have you ever been to a frolic?"

"Hmm?" Rose Rita asked. "Um. Once, last year."

"Was it wonderful?"

Rose Rita was glad the room was dark. Her face was burning hot, and she knew she was blushing. Darn it, why did she have to bring up the subject of dancing? Maybe it was a pleasant one for Hilda, but Rose Rita didn't care if she never went to a dance or even talked about one for the rest of her life. However, she said, "It was all right, I guess. I just—" She broke off. The idea was to cheer Hilda up, not to complain. "It was all right," Rose Rita said again.

"What happened?" Hilda asked. "Tell me all about it. What did everyone wear? Where was the frolic?"

"Well, it was in the school gymnasium. There was a band, and everyone dressed up."

"What is a gymnasium?"

"Uh, it's a building that our school has for games and things when, uh, it's too cold to go outside. It's very cold where I come from." Rose Rita pondered whether or not to throw in polar bears wandering the streets of New Zebedee in the winter time, but before she could make up her mind whether or not this would be a good touch, Hilda had another question.

"What did you wear?"

Rose Rita sighed. She was in for it now. She described the pink party dress that her mother had bought for her, down to every flounce and lace. Rose Rita hadn't been any too sure about that dress. With all the frills and lace it was just too girlish for her to feel comfortable in it. But she had worn it, and her description of it thrilled Hilda.

"It sounds so pretty! You must have danced with every boy there!" Hilda said.

"Umm, no." Rose Rita sighed again. "In fact, I didn't dance at all. I was a wallflower." Then she had to explain what that meant: She had been one of the girls who stood against the wall, waiting for a boy to ask her to dance. Only no boy had done that. Lewis had been there, standing across the gym floor with a bunch of other boys, and Rose Rita had tried to signal to him that she wanted to dance at least *once*, for crying out loud. But Lewis kept looking away, and in the end neither of them danced at all. Rose Rita had been so mad that she had hardly spoken to Lewis for more than a week, and even after that she had never once talked to him about the humiliating dance.

"Don't be too hard on your friend Lewis. Maybe he doesn't know how to dance," Hilda said when Rose Rita had finished the whole ghastly story.

By that time Rose Rita was really awake, because just telling the story had made her angry all over again. "I never thought of that," she admitted, surprised that she hadn't.

"You ought to offer to teach him," Hilda murmured. "Then he wouldn't be so bashful next time." Her voice trailed off, and soon she was asleep.

But now Rose Rita couldn't go to sleep. She lay awake brooding about the dance and about how she had yelled at her mother when she got home afterward. "I hate dances!" she had shouted. "Dances are stupid and dresses are stupid, and I'm never going again!" And she had crammed the pretty dress down in the very bottom of the hamper. Her mother had washed and ironed it, but Rose Rita had refused to wear it again. The pink dress was still hanging in her closet, next to all her sweatshirts and jeans.

Or rather it would be hanging there, in about one hundred twenty-three years, Rose Rita realized. Despite all her problems she could not help smiling. She had worked herself up so much over the stupid dance that she had almost forgotten all the trouble that she and Mrs. Zimmermann were in. She snuggled deeper into the bed, and with the warm quilts over her and the regular sound of Hilda's breathing lulling her, she eventually fell asleep.

CHAPTER NINE

On March 17 the moon was new. By that time Mrs. Zimmermann had recovered enough to help around the house. The Weiss family was delighted to learn what Rose Rita had known all along: Mrs. Zimmermann was a terrific cook. She taught Mrs. Weiss a delicious strudel recipe, and she did wonders with roast pork, chicken pie, and best of all, spice cake. The whole Weiss family praised her dishes to the skies, and Mrs. Weiss was grateful to be able to do more talking and less cooking than normal. Mrs. Zimmermann proved to be a good listener too, never running out of patience before Mrs. Weiss's torrent of words. And she had enough lingering magic to follow Grampa Drexel's weakly whispered directions in preparing herbal remedies for him. He did not improve much, but at least the old man held his own.

On Monday night, March 17, Rose Rita had a moment to talk with Grampa Drexel, who felt just well enough to sit in his rocking chair before the kitchen fire. She admitted miserably that her big idea of discovering the motive behind the gossip about the Weiss family had not worked out. And she asked the old man if he felt able to go ahead with the preparation of Mrs. Zimmermann's magical charm. "It has to be a secret," Rose Rita said. "So please don't tell her that I asked."

The old man sat with a blanket around his bony shoulders. His face was thinner than ever, and his hands shook all the time. He whispered, "It means a great deal to you, to have your friend's magic restored."

Rose Rita nodded. Then she took a deep breath and added, "But I don't want you to try anything that would hurt you. So if you're too weak to make the crystal, then—then—" Rose Rita had to swallow. "Then I guess you'd better not try."

The old man gave her a weary smile. "We shall see," he murmured. "On Thursday night the moon should be just right. A crystal prepared in its light will grow in power, as the crescent moon grows in size. So if we have a clear night, I will try. If the night is cloudy—well, we shall try again next month."

Rose Rita nodded miserably. If they failed this time, she knew it would signal the failure of their mission to keep the Weisses from being driven from their farm, and so Grampa Weiss would never have a second chance.

Tuesday was blustery, with sleet and freezing rain, and Rose Rita's heart sank. Wednesday was a day of low, ragged, gray clouds rushing overhead, and she was miserable. But then at about noon on Thursday the sun peeked out through a few jagged breaks in the clouds. The clouds began to blow away, and by late afternoon the sky was clear and blue. She began to hope that everything just might turn out all right, after all.

That evening Grampa Drexel asked Rose Rita to help him upstairs. She did, and at his direction she went to the room where he had showed her the crystal and got it for him. He stood at the big window at the west end of the hall. Lingering in the purple sky to the west was a skinny crescent moon, its horns pointed up. "I will work the charm here," he said. "You must help me prepare."

He gave her a flat piece of chalk and told her to draw a circle on the wooden floor. Rose Rita followed his directions. Then he showed her a paper with a design on it, like one of the hex symbols she had seen. This one had three circles inside a big circle, and each small circle had a strange word written inside it. Rose Rita faithfully copied the design. "Good," Grampa Drexel said. "Now you must leave me here for a quarter of an hour. Come back then and we will see what we will see."

That was a long fifteen minutes. Rose Rita went downstairs and helped Mrs. Weiss, who bustled about cleaning the kitchen. "Rose Rita, you are as nervous as a cat tonight," she said. "*Ach*, you would think that a young man was coming to court you, and you not ready yet! Sweep the crumbs from the counter, please. Oh, the troubles we are having. Today Mrs. Pilcher refused to sell me eggs and told me the farmers are talking about running us out of our home. Imagine! *Ach*, good fortune comes in teaspoons and bad luck comes in gallons, as my mother always said. No, dear, the spoons in this drawer, please. I was saying to Hermann only yesterday—"

Somehow or other Rose Rita got through the quarter hour without screaming. Then she hurried upstairs. Grampa Drexel leaned against the windowsill. He nodded feebly to her as she helped him to his room. In the yellow light of an oil lantern she saw a stack of books on a desk there. Once again they reminded Rose Rita of the ones she had seen at Mr. Stoltzfuss's house. And once again, as soon as the thought came to Rose Rita, she felt sleepy and confused and unable to speak. But Grampa Drexel noticed that she was staring at the books. "I have been reading a little about *erdspiegel*s," he said as he tapped the top book. "Albertus Magnus, this one.

I've marked a passage about mirrors. If I had more strength—"

He reeled, and Rose Rita helped him to the bed. He sat on the edge of the mattress and handed Rose Rita the little crystal sphere. "There," he said. "The spell has started, but it has made me tired. I must rest now. Remember, to gain full power, it must be buried in the earth for seven years. Longer to give it more power. Bury it tomorrow night, when the moon is in the sky again. I—I must rest."

Rose Rita realized that the effort of enchanting the crystal had been almost too much for the old man. She ran into the hallway and got down on her knees to erase the chalk circles. When she stood up, she held the crystal in her palms and stared into it. At its heart a tiny crescent shape glowed, just like the moon. It was a pale purple, Mrs. Zimmermann's favorite color.

Slipping away from the Weiss farm was difficult, but it could be managed, as Rose Rita discovered the next evening. She had thought hard about the problem of burying the crystal, and at last she had come up with an idea that might work. She bundled up warmly, took a lantern when no one was looking, and hurried away from the farm.

It was a long, cold walk. However, she was glad to find that her ankle seemed completely well again. At last she arrived at her destination, long past sunset. The moon was still in the sky, though it was low on the horizon and was beginning to turn red. It was still a crescent, but a little fatter than it had been the night before. Rose Rita looked all around until she found a good place. She had smuggled a large spoon out of the Weiss kitchen. She used it to dig away the thin crust of melting snow and to scoop up earth. The weather was cold but not freezing, and the soggy ground was soft. The crystal went into a special resting place, and on top of it went the soil that Rose Rita had dug up. She packed dirt around the enchanted globe until it was well buried, and then she studied the landscape carefully, memorizing landmarks. Using the spoon, she made some marks that she thought would help her later. She ruined the spoon, but she told herself that this was a price that had to be paid if her plan was to work.

She hurried back to the Weiss farm under a starry sky, the lantern throwing a yellow circle of light around her. For the first time she realized exactly how dark a country night could be, especially when there were no neon motel signs or stoplights or streetlamps to light the way. The stars helped a little, but their light was cold and feeble. The wind rustled in the trees, and now and then a distant dog howled, making her walk a little faster. At last she saw the warm, yellow windows of the Weiss house far ahead, and she walked faster than ever.

Rose Rita was abreast of the great dark shape that was Cottage Rock when she saw something strange. A pale-bluish light glowed at the foot of the rock. Not a bright light like a flashlight or even a candle, but a soft radiance. She was a little afraid, but she was more curious than frightened. So she left the road and crunched over the old snow until she reached Cottage Rock. On the snow at her feet lay an open book. Rose Rita stooped and picked it up, wondering why on earth it was here. The Weisses had only a few books, aside from the ones in Grampa Drexel's room, and they took good care of them. Books were scarce and expensive for a farm family.

The volume was large and flat, and it was so awkward to hold that Rose Rita could not manage to lift her lantern high enough to get a good look at it. But her eye fell on the first few words of the left-hand page:

> *Incantas brevoort diabolicus malificum zerstoren mickle gehent.*

Rose Rita frowned. She knew a little French, and Jonathan had taught her a little Latin, but this was not in either of them, although some of the words were Latin. And it did not look like the German words she had seen in the *fraktur* writing framed and hung like mottos on the walls of the Weiss house. In fact it did not look like any real language. Rose Rita wondered how she was even able to read in the darkness—but then she realized that the letters themselves were luminous. They were the source of the book's faint blue glow.

She read a few more words and found them puzzling

and nonsensical. She really ought to take the book to Grampa Drexel, to see what he could make of it. But maybe if she read a little more, she would understand. Sometimes the odd words *almost* seemed to make some kind of sense. Rose Rita read the whole page. When she had finished the last two words, *principium istum*, she felt a change in the air around her.

Rose Rita tried to tear her gaze away from the page. She could not. She was trapped! She remembered Grampa Drexel's warning about magical books—but now it was too late. She had started reading this one, and she could not stop!

The night around her grew thicker, darker. She dropped the lantern, and its light went out. The black shape of Cottage Rock reared before her. Rose Rita felt that something malevolent waited there now, up atop the rock ten feet above her head. She could not visualize it, but she knew that some demonic *thing* was beginning to take shape, forming out of thin air. She felt its anger and its hatred. The words she was reading were bringing this awful being into the world—and it could not wait to tear her limb from limb.

Rose Rita could not stop reading. She began the top of the next page. With every effort she could muster, she tried to rip her gaze away from the page. She could succeed only in slowing down her pace. By the time she was halfway down the page, she heard a deep, snuffling grunt from above her. Then a horrible, hissing laugh, mocking and eager. Hot breath blew against the back of her neck. It smelled of decay and brimstone, like rotten eggs. Her hair prickled. She could almost feel a taloned hand reaching down from above her, hovering in the darkness just over her head, ready to snatch her up the moment she finished reading the spell. She wanted to scream, to run, to throw the book away. Held by the deadly enchantment, she could do none of these things.

Her mind raced furiously. Grampa Drexel had said something about how you escaped from this kind of spell. What was it? A smart person could get out of the trap—if he took every step backward! That was it! But what did that mean? She had not been walking as she read, but standing still.

Rose Rita heard a slithery, wet sound. Something big was licking its terrible lips. Liquid dropped hissing into the snow. The thing forming on the rock was drooling, and its spittle was hot enough to boil. She was almost to the end of the third page! From the corner of her eye she saw that the print ended at the very top of the next page! Another sickening burst of hot stench rolled over her—

Then Rose Rita got an idea. She began to read *backward.* Word by word, she found she could slowly work her way back up the page. It got easier as she went along. She had a sense of great hostility and frustration from the creature on the rock, but this grew less and less. She read backward up the second page, and then the first. At last she came to the first words she had noticed, but now she went through them in reverse:

gehent mickle zerstoren malificum diabolicus
brevoort Incantas.

The book writhed like a snake in her hands! She flung it away—and it burst into flame! Rose Rita jumped back. Before the book even touched the ground, a hot, white flame had consumed it. She was free!

With a shaking hand she reached down and picked up the lantern she had dropped. She had no way of relighting it, and she was in darkness. But she knew somehow that Cottage Rock was just a rock again, and no malevolent demon crouched upon it, waiting to devour her. Despite her great fear Rose Rita sternly forced herself to wait until she had control of herself again. Then she walked in a determined way straight for the Weiss house. Rose Rita had the feeling that this episode was not like the books in Stoltzfuss's house. No spell would prevent her from talking about her experience. But she also knew that she did not want to talk about it—not yet. She had stupidly done the very thing that Grampa Drexel had warned her against. She was angry. Angry at herself, and angry at the person who had left the book. For she knew that someone had deliberately tried to kill her or one of the Weisses by leaving the book at the foot of Cottage Rock, where Heinrich and the other children often played. Now Rose Rita was more determined than ever to get to the bottom of this nefarious evil. And she would help the Weisses, and Grampa Drexel, and Mrs. Zimmermann too!

Though she was breathing hard, she got back to the farm safely, and when Mrs. Weiss scolded her for frightening them all, she apologized and said that she just had to go for a long walk to clear her mind. Hilda looked at her uncertainly, and Heinrich scowled. Somehow, talking with Rose Rita and plotting things with her had made him feel braver than he used to be. He clearly resented missing whatever adventure she had embarked on.

But worst of all Mrs. Zimmermann gave Rose Rita a long, sad look. It almost broke her heart, but Rose Rita could not tell her friend what she had been up to. She went to bed that night confused and upset.

As for Mrs. Zimmermann, she felt almost well again. It troubled her that she still could not remember very much about how they had arrived in this strange place and time, or even a great deal about the mirror. Still, while Mr. Drexel nursed her back to health and then later when she took her turn and ministered to him, she had learned a thing or two. If Rose Rita had secrets that she wasn't telling, Mrs. Zimmermann had a few too. In fact the reason that Grampa Drexel had been studying the magical prescriptions of Albertus Magnus was that he and Mrs. Zimmermann were researching magic mirrors.

These were dangerous, as Mrs. Zimmermann had inadvertently discovered. According to what Mr. Drexel learned, an enchanted mirror could literally be a way of inviting spirits, either good or evil ones, to our world. One evening as he finished his supper, Grampa Drexel asked Mrs. Zimmermann where she had found this mirror, and whether she knew much about its magic. "No," she had replied slowly. "I didn't even know that the mirror *was* a magic one for the longest time. As I recall, I found it in a junk store about twenty years ago. I like to pick through junk stores and collect odd items, and this mirror just seemed to cry out to me. It was old, scratched, and dim, but I bought it for fifty cents and took it home and cleaned it up. It has hung in my house for ages, and until about two or three months ago I never had any trouble with it."

Grampa Drexel was sitting propped up in bed, and Mrs. Zimmermann sat in a chair beside him. She had been reading aloud to him from his magic texts, and the old man listened with closed eyes. "And then," he said, "you say the magic began with flashing lights, and you saw a ghost."

"Yes," Mrs. Zimmermann told him. "It was the ghost of the woman who first saw that I had some magic and showed me how to awaken it."

Grampa Drexel opened his eyes at that. "Strange," he murmured. "I always was taught that a woman's magic had to be started by a male wizard and vice versa. But

I have lived long enough to know that the ways of magic are devious. So. How much can you remember of the evil force?"

Mrs. Zimmermann shook her head. "Almost nothing. Just two hideous staring eyes, burning red, like coals of fire—ugh!" She shivered. "And I heard a sort of voice in my head, saying, 'Forget! Forget!' "

Grampa Drexel nodded. He reached for one of the books and leafed slowly through it. He found the page he was seeking and touched an illustration there. It was a sort of combination of letters, like this:

Grampa Drexel tapped the strange figure twice. "This was one of the things scratched in the back of your mirror. Do you know what it is?"

Mrs. Zimmermann shook her head. "I can see that it is a magical emblem of some sort, but I don't recognize it. My special field is talismans, not cabalistic insignia."

Grampa Drexel shook his head dolefully. "This mark is a symbol for the Enochian demon Aziel. He is an evil spirit who perverts and corrupts innocent earth magic."

Mrs. Zimmermann went pale. "I have heard of such beings. But I've never run across any like this. I guess my life was pretty quiet in New Zebedee."

"Ah. New Zebedee." Grampa Drexel closed the book and gave Mrs. Zimmermann a long, sorrowful look. "You have not told me the whole truth, Florence Zimmermann. You say you are from a place called New Zebedee; you say it is far to the west. But I know some geography, and I do not think such a place as New Zebedee exists."

Mrs. Zimmermann squirmed a bit. How could she tell this nice old man that the ghost in the mirror had been his own step-granddaughter, grown old and sour? Well, perhaps she could keep just a little back. She said, "I am not quite sure how to explain this. Rose Rita and I do come from New Zebedee, and it is a real town, but it was not settled until 1835."

Mr. Drexel frowned. "Then it does not yet exist. Are you telling me, Mrs. Zimmermann, that you somehow from the future have come?"

"Yes," Mrs. Zimmermann admitted. "From quite a long way in the future."

"*Ach,*" Mr. Drexel said. He looked thoughtful. "I will not ask more. It is dangerous for a wizard to know much about the future."

Mrs. Zimmermann was surprised that the old man accepted her story so readily. But then he was a wizard, and wizards have a way of taking in stride fantastic ideas that might knock a mail carrier or a lawyer for a loop.

After a long time Grampa Drexel said, "This is what I think. I think you bought a mirror that had been enchanted by an evil sorcerer, a real *hexer*. Perhaps he himself has long been dead—in your time. But I think he is alive in this time, our time. And I believe that his power over the mirror is so great because this is also *his* time." The old man held up a long, bony finger. "However, Albertus has more to say about *erdspiegel*s that are created by means of Aziel's infernal powers. Aziel sometimes helps his followers find riches, but he is a very dangerous spirit who often demands human sacrifice in payment for his aid. And like all evil spirits Aziel is tricky, spiteful, and vicious. There may be a chance, just a chance, you understand, that the evil spirit would reveal the master of the mirror to us. In doing so he would be performing an act of great treachery—but that is exactly what demons do."

"Yes," Mrs. Zimmermann said sadly. "I see the chance that you mean. Only neither of us is strong enough to try to use my mirror. Why, if the wizard who controls it became aware of us, he might take away our memory for good, or make both of us drooling idiots."

Grampa Drexel nodded wearily. "You are right. If I had my full health, I would chance it. But the least exertion exhausts me. However, there is my granddaughter, Hilda. You may have noticed that she has powers of her own. Oh, they are not developed yet, but she will be a great *braucher* in time. We may be able to call upon her strength to aid us."

Mrs. Zimmermann shook her head. "No. I can't allow

Hilda to run such a terrible risk. We'll have to think of something else."

After taking a deep breath Grampa Drexel said, "I must admit that I am relieved. Little Hilda is dear to me, as dear as a grandchild by blood would be. Well, I have written out the necessary charm, translating from Albertus Magnus. There it is, that piece of paper folded in the book. Let me try to recover my strength, and perhaps before the moon is full we may be able to make an attempt. Or else we must of something else think, as you say."

Mrs. Zimmermann gathered up the tray with Grampa Drexel's supper dishes on it. Neither of them noticed a soft squeak as someone moved in the hall. It was Heinrich, and he had been sitting on the floor just outside his grandfather's door. He had heard everything that Mrs. Zimmermann and Grampa Drexel had said, and now he couldn't wait to find Rose Rita and share it with her.

CHAPTER TEN

Heinrich went straight to Rose Rita and told her what he had heard. When he had finished, he gave her a look of awe. "Are you really from the future?" he asked.

Rose Rita frowned and shrugged. "It's no big deal. It's like meeting someone from Persia or Timbuktoo."

"*Ach*, I see."

"But you have to promise not to tell anyone. It's a secret."

Heinrich promised, and Rose Rita trusted him. But when she told him what she thought they ought to do, his eyes widened and he refused. He could get used to the idea of time-traveling visitors, but he wanted nothing to do with magic mirrors and hex wizards. Despite Rose

Rita's efforts Heinrich resisted her suggestions. Then, on March 27 Papa Weiss came into the house with a long face. "Now even the minister says we are no longer welcome, because so many people think we have something to do with evil witchcraft. We will move," he muttered. "We cannot live where people hate us so badly. We will move to my brother's place in Harrisburg and try to sell this farm, so we can begin again elsewhere." And he set the date for moving for April 1, the day on which Grampa Drexel was fated to fall ill.

The next days were frantic ones of packing. Mrs. Weiss alternately bawled at being forced to leave her home and rattled on, telling long stories about every stick of furniture. Heinrich grew weepy and talked about how much he would miss his "fort," which was what he called Cottage Rock. Rose Rita took advantage of this, telling Heinrich that his family might be able to stay if the two of them could just put her plan into action. Slowly she won Heinrich over, and finally, in the twilight of the family's last day on the farm, he listened to her one more time.

"You really think we could stay?" he asked in a hopeful voice.

"Sure," Rose Rita replied. "And if you can use the crazy mirror to find the treasure too, your family wouldn't ever have to worry about moving again. They don't make rich people move off their land, no matter how weird they may act."

"Yes, that's true," Heinrich said slowly. "I've been trying and trying to figure out the code in the *fraktur* writing just for that reason."

"Sure," Rose Rita said. "I've been trying too, but there has to be an easier way. So get that paper from your grampa's book, and I'll get the mirror, and we'll give it a try."

"But you're not a *braucher* witch," Heinrich objected.

Rose Rita snorted. "Look, the mirror itself is magic, right? If it's magic, then you don't have to be magic to use it." Rose Rita took a deep breath. She had one last card to play, and she was pretty sure it would work. Rose Rita remembered how fascinated Heinrich had been on first seeing her beanie. She had kept it in a drawer since her arrival at the farm, because she realized it would be hard to explain to people in 1828 what the little colored buttons meant. They were pins with cartoon characters enameled on them, and she had gotten them years ago from Kellogg's cereals, but none of the cartoons existed in 1828. "Look," she said to Heinrich, "if you'll get the paper, I'll give you that hat of mine that you liked."

Heinrich's eyes grew thoughtful. Rose Rita knew that they had a deal. About twenty minutes later, just about at sunset, Heinrich brought the paper to the barn, and Rose Rita brought the mirror. It was easier than she had thought to sneak it out, because the whole house was in such a turmoil of packing and preparing. She hung the mirror on a nail, and Heinrich handed her the paper. She gave him the beanie in exchange, and with a proud smile he tugged it onto his head. Rose Rita felt a little stab of regret. That beanie was like an old friend of hers, but a bargain was a bargain, and besides, right now the paper was far more important to her plans.

Rose Rita studied it. "We have to draw a circle," she said. "Then there are certain words I must chant. It says here that only those in the circle will be protected, so we'd better make it a large one."

The barn had a stone floor, and the unused stall was clear of straw. Rose Rita drew the circle, using chalk. It was a lot like the one she had helped Grampa Drexel draw, but there were differences too. This time it was a double circle with a five-pointed star in the center of it. "We have to be sure a single point is to the east," Rose Rita said, reading from the paper. "That way it will be a good symbol and not an evil one."

"East is that way," Heinrich said, pointing. "The sun comes up right behind the tree on that side of the house."

Then there were more outlandish words to print. Rose Rita did these very carefully, and checked them twice to make sure they were accurate. When everything was complete, Rose Rita and Heinrich stood in the center of the star she had drawn. For a moment she hesitated, remembering the last time she had read from a book of magic. That time she had almost summoned a ravenous demon. But the thought made her more angry than scared, and more determined than ever to go through with her plan.

In a firm voice she began to read the invocation on the paper that Heinrich had brought. Rose Rita did not want to look at the mirror, so she kept her gaze on the paper.

"*Ach!*" Heinrich said in a hoarse whisper. "The mirror is flashing!"

Rose Rita looked. The mirror was shimmering with a pale, light-blue glow. At first she could see the two of them reflected in it, Heinrich's face looking over her left shoulder. Then a strange thing happened. The mirror went dark. It was like a TV screen being turned off: First there was an image, and then there was only a blankness. But the weird light continued to flicker around the edge of the darkness. Then, slowly, another image began to form. It was a tall, skinny man, standing behind something low, rounded, and white. The features were at first indistinct, but they gradually grew clearer. Heinrich stirred beside Rose Rita, as if he were about to step out of the circle, but she felt the movement and pinched his arm hard. The man was holding something long and thin. He stooped over and started to work.

Rose Rita gasped. The man had a shovel, and he was digging. And the white thing in front of him was a gravestone. Carved on it was the name *Diedrich Hoffmann* and the figures *1767–1828*. Beyond the man was a white church, its steeple ghostly against the darkening evening sky. Rose Rita felt there was something awfully familiar about the scene, and about the figure. But she could not recognize him, because the man's face was averted as he dug into the hard, cold earth. Suddenly, the digging man stiffened. He turned and glared around him.

"*Stoltzfuss!*" Heinrich shrieked.

The eyes blazed out at them, and Rose Rita screamed. She had seen those eyes late on a cold night, when the same bony figure had been out in the yard beneath the moon. Now they seemed to rip at her mind. The mirror flared one last time, and then it fell dark.

Rose Rita's mind whirled. She felt as if her brain had been scrambled.

"That was the Good Shepherd Lutheran Church," Heinrich whispered. "It is only a few miles from here!"

In the mirror Rose Rita could see only her own scared face and Heinrich's looking back from the glass. She took a deep breath. "I think we ought to go there," she said.

"Yes," Heinrich said. His voice was strangely dreamy. "We can stop him from digging up the dead if we go now."

Rose Rita nodded. "Get the horse," she said.

Heinrich saddled Nicklaus, and both of them climbed up onto the animal's back. Rose Rita could ride pretty well, but Heinrich was better, so she sat behind him. They clopped out into the twilight, and Heinrich kept the pace slow until they were well out of earshot. Then the horse walked faster.

Rose Rita felt her head buzzing oddly. She knew their only hope was to go to the graveyard and confront Stoltzfuss and— What? There ought to be something else, but she could not for the life of her think what it was. Oh, well, it would come to her once they got there. It never occurred to her that an evil spell was luring them to the churchyard.

It was a brisk night, with gusty wind and blowing snow. Before long they rode past fields crusted with glimmering ice, almost glowing in the darkness. Heinrich turned the horse right at a fork in the road. Minutes later the church they had seen loomed into view, and they could dimly see a great ugly black hole in the snow covering the churchyard—the place where Stoltzfuss had been digging.

Nicklaus stopped, whickering nervously. Rose Rita slipped off, and then Heinrich followed. Both of them walked toward the open grave. Rose Rita swallowed. She remembered the terrible nightmare about the cemetery where the skeletons had come clawing out of their graves. What if there were a corpse inside that hole, moldy and hollow eyed and grinning? And what if two fleshless arms should shoot out and grab her? Nonsense, she told herself. Graves went deep, and this hole was barely started, because the pile of dirt beside it was small. In fact—

A strong hand closed on her shoulder. "Ah," a creaky voice said. "So I was right. Some little birds were spying on me. And here they both are! Turn around!"

Rose Rita's throat closed, and her jaw felt as if it were frozen shut. She could not scream, but her heart was pounding wildly. The voice carried an undeniable command, and it compelled her to turn around. Heinrich turned too.

Old Stoltzfuss stood over them, grinning in evil triumph. "You have saved me a great deal of work," he said. "Digging up a body is no joke when the ground is frozen! But fresh ingredients are always better. You will come with me!"

Rose Rita tried to run away, but her legs were like lead. She heard the horse break into a gallop. Stoltzfuss cursed aloud. "Fool that I am, I should have cast my spell to cover the beast as well as you two. No matter. No one will know where to look for you, and they will never find you." He noticed Rose Rita twitching, and he laughed nastily. "Don't bother. I cast a strong enchantment over my two spies. This time it does much more than just silence you! You can move only when I tell you to, as long as I am not concentrating on any other magic. And now both of you will get into my wagon and lie quietly while I take us to a place more suited for my purposes."

And they did. Rose Rita felt as though cold, invisible hands made her arms and legs move. She and Heinrich lay side by side in the back of the wagon, with Stoltzfuss's tall back towering before them and the stinging snowflakes falling on their foreheads and cheeks. The wagon rumbled along for what seemed like an eternity to Rose Rita. She had had nightmares before that were like this, when she wanted desperately to move but could not. She knew that something terrible was going to happen, and she hoped that the horse would find its way back to the house and that Mrs. Zimmermann could somehow guess where they had been taken.

At last the wagon creaked to a halt, and once more the unseen hands forced her muscles to move. She, Heinrich, and Stoltzfuss walked into the Stoltzfuss farmhouse, down a long, gloomy corridor, and into the room decorated with hex symbols. A lone black candle burned on the big table in the center of the room. On the table were the black sword and the brass incense burner she had seen before, and two mirrors—one of them a twin to the one that still hung in the Weiss barn.

Stoltzfuss left Heinrich and Rose Rita standing like statues while he went elsewhere. He returned in a few moments with a chair and a coil of rope. "Boy," he said, "you sit."

Heinrich stiffly sat in the chair, and Stoltzfuss bound him with the rope, hand and foot, so that he could hardly stir. "I will have to break this enchantment while I prepare for a greater one," Stoltzfuss explained. "And I don't want you interfering with a mighty act of magic."

He pulled a large, turnip-shaped watch from his pocket and looked at it. "We have some time yet," he said. "These things have to be done just right, or they won't work at all. And this particular charm will work only if it is completed on the last stroke of midnight." For a moment he looked at them both, grinning in fierce triumph. Then he said, "I believe I will keep the charm on you for a while longer. I owe you both a debt of revenge. You, boy, are a member of the family that I most hate. And girl, your cleverness cost me a book of magic that is irreplaceable. It should have trapped and destroyed you, but somehow you knew the trick of reading backward, and so you destroyed it instead. You spies want to know what I was doing? I will tell you, since you will never live to use the knowledge!

"You must know that a great treasure is buried on the Weiss farm. Well, the treasure is rightfully mine! Long ago my father was a Hessian soldier serving the British in the Revolutionary War. His troop had the task of recovering traitors' gold from the town of Donniker. Three people stole it from my father's troop, and one of the thieves was Heinrich Weiss, this young villain's grandfather. Old Weiss succeeded in hiding the treasure, but my father caught him.

"So my father had captured a thief who had stolen from the British Crown. Did my father get a proper reward? Not at all! When the war ended, he went to prison! And there he brooded over the money that Heinrich Weiss had hidden, gold that should have been his. After he got out of prison, my father learned that Heinrich Weiss had died. He traced the Weiss family to this valley. Now, he had captured Weiss not far from this very spot, and he knew the gold had to be nearby. So he brought my mother and me over from Germany, and we bought this farm, and he watched the Weiss family, hoping they would lead him to the treasure."

Rose Rita squirmed—not much, but she managed to wriggle her toes and fingers. Old Stoltzfuss was getting all wrapped up in his wild story of treasure and revenge. She thought he must have a screw loose somewhere. The missing money might have belonged to the town of Donniker, or to the American army, but any way she looked at it, the gold certainly did not belong to Stoltzfuss's father. However, Stoltzfuss obviously believed it did, and because of his anger and greed, his concentration was wandering from the spell that held them prisoner. She hoped that the charm would wear off, and that she could do—well, *something*. Maybe dive through the closed window and run away. Or break the mirror, or grab the black sword that lay on the table.

The angry Stoltzfuss paced the floor on his spidery legs. His grating, high-pitched voice grew louder. "I always hated this backwoods place. By rights I should be rich! But the accursed Weiss family kept the treasure from my family. My father never learned where the gold lay. When he died, I found other ways to discover such things."

He pointed to the table. "I studied hex magic. I found an old woman to teach me how to begin, and then I read books that she had never even heard of! I had to sell most of my wretched land to get money to make those two mirrors. Then it took me years to discover how to summon and control the earth demon Aziel. I am a clever man, my young spies. It takes cunning to deal with Aziel."

Rose Rita thought she could walk again if she tried. But she didn't dare try yet, not with old Stoltzfuss so close. If he would only start to pace again, she thought—

Stoltzfuss picked up and fondled a black-bound book. "So on my side I have Aziel, and my magic, and my wonderful mirrors."

Heinrich burst out: "Why didn't you use your old mirrors and let us alone?"

Stoltzfuss started. "So," he said, "I have been inattentive, eh? Let me strengthen the charm." He put down the book and waved his bony fingers while chanting something.

Rose Rita felt her knees stiffening again. Darn Heinrich, anyway! He had to speak up, just when she was about to make a break for it!

After a moment Stoltzfuss said, "Now you are quiet,

eh? How you glare at me! You may hate me for what I am going to do, but I don't care. Your grandfather and father thwarted my family's chance for riches and respect, so I despise you.

"Foolish boy, you ask why I did not use the mirrors. I did use them! But your farm is large. I have come there for three years now, once each month when the moon is right, but each night I can cover only a small bit of ground. I have found no treasure—and always I have had to flee like a thief if a dog barked or someone came out with a lantern. But if your family moved off the farm, then I could have all the time I need." Stoltzfuss laughed. "It is easy to convince people that a wicked sorcerer is burning schools and changing the weather—especially when a sorcerer *is* doing those things! The fools I turned against old Drexel never guessed that *I* was the magician, not your doddering old relative!"

Stoltzfuss looked at his watch again. "You could have left me alone, but you had to come spying. Your family could have moved months ago, but you stayed and stayed. Too bad for you! You see, I have borrowed money against my house and land, and on April first, I must pay the mortgage on what remains of my poor farm or lose it. I am out of time, and so are you!"

The wizard lowered his voice, sounding nearly as frightened as Rose Rita felt: "I know a dangerous magic spell to make Aziel reveal the hiding place of treasure. I must use the larger mirror to open up a gateway to Aziel's plane of existence, and I must put the question to him."

His crooked, stained teeth showed in a wolfish grimace. "Aziel demands tribute for such information, human blood and hearts. I was digging up a dead body for him—but here *you* are! The first heart will be yours, girl. And the second one will be the boy's. I am sure that Aziel will appreciate a little extra sacrifice. Now I must prepare. The spell begins just before midnight." The terrible old man held his watch so that Heinrich and Rose Rita could see its face. "The two of you have not quite three hours to live!"

CHAPTER ELEVEN

Mrs. Zimmermann missed Rose Rita at about ten o'clock that night. She asked Hilda if she had seen her, and Hilda shook her head. Mrs. Zimmermann helped the Weiss family fold and pack sheets for a few more minutes, but she had a nagging feeling that something just wasn't right. It was hard to explain, but she had a kind of sixth sense about trouble that she had kept even after losing her witchy powers. Right now that sixth sense was screaming at the back of her mind, telling her that Rose Rita was in trouble and that she had to act fast.

So she took a lantern and went outside. Before long she peeked into the barn. What she saw made her gasp. There on the floor was a magic circle, inexpertly but accurately drawn, and there hanging on a nail beside the stable door was her mirror. Something rustled across the stone floor in the breeze from the open door. Mrs. Zimmermann stepped inside and picked it up. It was the magic incantation that Grampa Drexel had translated from Albertus Magnus. It didn't take Mrs. Zimmermann long to put two and two together. She still did not know where Rose Rita had gone, but she had a good idea of where she had started from. Mrs. Zimmermann went back inside, asked Hilda to come with her, and went up to Grampa Drexel's room.

The old man was very weak. His breath came in painful gasps. In a few words Mrs. Zimmermann told him about what she had found. "I will try to help," he murmured, but he could not even sit up in bed.

"No," Mrs. Zimmermann said. "I know that Hilda has powers too. I hate to ask, but I need her help. I want her to use the mirror with me to find out what has happened to Rose Rita."

After a terrible moment the old man nodded. "Yes," he said. "I am sorry, my dear Hilda. It must be. I lack the strength, and even with the protection of the magic circle, anyone who has no magic would run a grave risk of being detected and trapped by the maker of this infernal mirror. If you are brave enough, dear Hilda, you must try."

"I will try," Hilda said. She went to her room and

brought the crystal that she had showed to Rose Rita, and then she and Mrs. Zimmermann went out to the barn. They carefully stepped inside the magic circle. With Mrs. Zimmermann's hands firm on her shoulder Hilda began to recite the magic spell. In her own hands she cupped the crystal ball. It began to shimmer with a beautiful rose-pink glow. Soon the mirror had picked up the color and shimmered pink too. That was reassuring to Mrs. Zimmermann, who could remember that the evil power in the mirror had had a cold, blue aura, not a warm, living, pink one.

Then the mirror darkened and cleared, as it had done once before that evening. "Oh!" Mrs. Zimmermann said.

It showed a frightening scene. In a room painted in hex symbols, Heinrich Weiss was tied to a chair. A tall, thin man stood before a square mirror, a twin of the one on the stable wall. And worst of all, lying on a table before the man was Rose Rita, her eyes wide, staring, and terrified. The man seemed to be chanting, though the two could hear no sound.

"It is Mr. Stoltzfuss!" Hilda said.

The mirror went blank, and the rosy light died. After a moment Mrs. Zimmermann strode out of the magic circle and grabbed the mirror. "Come on," she said. "You and I have to get over there. Where's your father?"

Hilda shook her head. "He and my brothers have gone to the next town to buy a larger wagon," she said.

"No one in Steinbrücke would sell them one, and I don't know when he will come back. It may not be until tomorrow morning."

"Then it's just the two of us." Mrs. Zimmermann tucked the mirror under her arm. "Is there a buggy or a wagon we could take?"

"*Ja,*" Hilda said. "The buggy is not yet loaded with the things we are moving. But Papa has the horses, and the mule is too stubborn to pull the cart after dark!"

The two left the barn on foot—only to meet Nicklaus in the farmyard. The big chestnut horse had left the cold churchyard and come straight home. Thanking her stars that she had learned about horses and wagons when she was young, Mrs. Zimmermann soon had him hitched to the buggy. She put the mirror in and climbed up. Hilda came after her. "It may be dangerous," Mrs. Zimmermann warned. "That was black magic if I ever saw it!"

"I don't care," Hilda said. "Heinrich is my brother and Rose Rita is my friend. We have to help them."

Following Hilda's directions, Mrs. Zimmermann urged the horse along the dark road. Nicklaus was very tired, and the night was cold, and he was not enthusiastic about pulling the buggy, so they made only slow progress. It was past eleven when they topped the hill overlooking the Stoltzfuss farm. By that time the wind and snow had increased. Mrs. Zimmermann could see that they were in for a real blizzard.

"It's down there," Hilda said. "See the light?"

Sure enough, a dim reddish square showed in the night—lamplight or candlelight shining through a window of the Stoltzfuss house. Mrs. Zimmermann urged the horse off the side of the road and tied him to a small tree. "We'll have to be very careful and very quiet," she said as she and Hilda started down the hill.

It was slow going in the dark night. An owl hooted dismally over and over, and off in the distance a melancholy dog howled. The cold wind whistled mournfully through the bare trees, and more snow fell on the icy sheet that still lay on the fields. Mrs. Zimmermann shivered from more than the cold. The frosty-blue glimmer of the crusted snow reminded her of the flashes of light she had seen just before the red eyes had tried to blast her memory away. She still carried her mirror, and she noticed that it was shimmering with faint gleams of blue light too. She turned its face away from her and Hilda, just in case.

They came quietly up to the house and circled it. One window had a shade pulled, but a little light leaked from the edge, where the shade was not quite wide enough to cover the entire window. Mrs. Zimmermann edged up to this and peeked in.

What she saw made her heart feel icy cold. The scene was just as it had been in the mirror. Rose Rita lay rigid on the table. Beyond her, Heinrich, tied and gagged, struggled against the ropes that bound him to a chair.

With his arms lifted, Stoltzfuss chanted something. She could not see what he was speaking to, but it seemed to be about eye level and off to the left. Mrs. Zimmermann made the grim guess that he had hung his own mirror up on the wall and was incanting to it, opening a pathway between this world and the terrible domain of the demons. From her studies she knew very well that such dark deeds were best performed at midnight. And it was almost midnight!

"Come on," she whispered to Hilda. They crept around to the back of the house. Mrs. Zimmermann tried the doorknob, but the door was securely locked. "Get out that crystal," she said to Hilda. "I have a spell for you to work."

Hilda, shivering beside her, took out the crystal. Its light was friendly and warm, still a lovely rose pink. "What do I do?"

Mrs. Zimmermann paused a moment. Then with a funny look at Hilda she said, "This was almost the first spell I ever learned. An old woman named Granny Wetherbee taught it to me. It's what a good witch uses to undo spells of binding cast by evil magicians—like the one keeping this door locked. Recite after me." And she began to whisper to Hilda the words of power that no longer worked for her.

Hilda repeated them, her voice quavering. At the last word the crystal flared up brighter, and a single thin ray shot out to touch the doorknob. When Mrs. Zimmermann tried it again, it turned in her hand and the door soundlessly opened.

Bending low, Mrs. Zimmermann whispered into Hilda's ear, "I'm going to try to bluff the old man. You have to help Heinrich get loose. Then whatever happens to me, you children run back to the buggy and go home as fast as you can. Don't wait!"

They slipped along the hall to a door through which flickering blue light showed. It was open, for old Stoltzfuss was confident that no one had any idea of what he was doing. Just as they got to the door, a clock began to bong somewhere in the house, a dreadful, fateful tolling. It was twelve o'clock, the witching hour!

Mrs. Zimmermann stepped inside the room and gasped. She heard Hilda stifle a cry beside her. They saw Stoltzfuss's back. Before him was Rose Rita, still lying faceup on the table. A huge knife was stuck into the wood beside her right leg. Beyond her, hanging on the wall, was a mirror that was the twin of Mrs. Zimmermann's. And in the mirror was a horrible *presence.*

Mrs. Zimmermann did not look directly at it, but she had an impression of ravenous hunger, of deep, dark evil, and of implacable hatred. She did not have to be told that she was in the presence of something demonic. Baleful power radiated from the dark image—flickering blue flashes like heat lightning on a restless summer night.

The clock was halfway through its twelve chimes.

Stoltzfuss had not even noticed the two slipping into the room. In a high, horrible, screechy voice he was crying out, "Aziel! Great Aziel! I offer you drink and food for the answer to my humble question! Tell me now, and you shall drink the wine that pleases you, and eat the flesh that strengthens you. *Where is the treasure I seek?*"

And something happened. Mrs. Zimmermann reeled. Hilda had slipped away to the right and was tearing at the ropes binding Heinrich, but Mrs. Zimmermann, behind Stoltzfuss, was in the path of Aziel's "answer." It was not expressed aloud, nor in any language that a human ear could hear, but it washed out in a great black wave of *feeling*. It had no meaning for Mrs. Zimmermann, but she vaguely heard Stoltzfuss cry out in triumph and glee. The last stroke of twelve sounded. Baleful red eyes, glowing like embers, stared out of the mirror on the wall, hungry and commanding and anciently evil.

Without thinking, Mrs. Zimmermann held up the mirror that she still carried, trying to shield herself from that hellish gaze. Instantly she felt the power of the demon ease, and she peeked cautiously around the edge of the mirror.

By accident she had held her mirror up so that it was exactly opposite Stoltzfuss's mirror on the wall. She saw that her mirror reflected his, and his reflected hers. There were an infinite number of glaring red eyes, reflected and reflected again, over and over. The dark power pouring out of the mirror on the wall was caught and sent back by hers.

And between the two was Stoltzfuss. He had already lifted the great knife high to strike. He was crying out something in a high, hawklike shriek. The knife began to plunge downward—

Clang! A flying, tumbling sword struck his arm, and the knife spun away into the air. Free of his bonds, Heinrich had snatched up the sword and thrown it spinning. He screamed, "Run, Rose Rita!"

"No!" Stoltzfuss grabbed for her arm, but Rose Rita had come to life! She rolled off the table and lunged away.

Dark, soundless laughter seemed to drink up all the light in the room. The mirror that Mrs. Zimmermann held pulled at her hands. It was like holding a powerful magnet that was being attracted by one equally powerful. But Mrs. Zimmermann did not know whether she should hold the mirror or let go of it.

For the first time Stoltzfuss seemed to realize that intruders had broken in on him. He whirled away from the mirror, shielding his eyes—only to be caught in the hate-filled red gaze of the leering demon reflected from Mrs. Zimmermann's mirror. He tried to run, but the same awful power that he had used to hold Rose Rita and Heinrich now gripped him. He screamed, "No! No! Don't take me! Take them, instead, I command you!"

The dark, silent laughter rolled again. Mrs. Zimmermann blinked. Stoltzfuss was *dissolving.* His body seemed to be pulled in two directions at once, and it was becoming misty, like black smoke. With a wailing scream he tried to cover his eyes.

Too late. His body suddenly was nothing more than a dark band of smoke connecting the two mirrors. Then the power of magic was too strong for Mrs. Zimmermann to resist. The mirror pulled free of her fingers, sped through the air, and smacked against the one on the wall. A soundless explosion of dire blue light flashed out—

And both mirrors disappeared without a trace.

Stoltzfuss was nowhere to be seen.

But—Mrs. Zimmermann shivered at the thought—no doubt Aziel the demon dined well that night.

CHAPTER TWELVE

"I thought we'd be home by now," Rose Rita complained.

Another whole week had passed. On the night that old Stoltzfuss had met his end, Rose Rita, Mrs. Zimmermann, Hilda, and Heinrich had struggled back through a raging snowstorm to the Weiss farm. They told the whole family about what the evil sorcerer had attempted to do. April 1 found the family practically snowbound, but the blizzard blew itself out in the afternoon. The next morning Mr. Weiss and some neighbors rode out to the Stoltzfuss farm. What they found there was more than enough to convince them all that Stoltzfuss, and not Grampa Drexel, was the evil magician who had been plaguing the community. They discovered books of black magic, and other magical paraphernalia, like black candles, human bones, and some wax figures. One of these resembled Grampa Drexel. When these images were brought to him, he took them and performed some cleansing ritual. The next morning Grampa Drexel was out of bed and looking far healthier than Mrs. Zimmermann and Rose Rita had ever seen him. The family later heard that three other people in the community who had been ailing made miraculous recoveries the same day.

As for Stoltzfuss, no trace of him could be found. Some thought that he had fled after his terrible deeds had been discovered. Others guessed the truth: that dark forces had stolen him away. The four people who really knew—Rose Rita, Mrs. Zimmermann, Hilda, and Heinrich—agreed it would be better never to tell the whole fantastic story. Many people might believe such a tale, but others would always think the four had lost their wits. Yet no matter what the people of the valley thought had happened to Mr. Stoltzfuss, they seemed to feel that his disappearance improved the community.

The weather improved too, that first week of April. The sun grew warm, and the snow really began to melt. The spring thaw was clearly upon them at last. At the end of the week a delegation of farmers and their wives came out to the Weiss farm with offerings of food and tearful apologies, which Mrs. Weiss apparently enjoyed more than anything else that she had experienced in a long while. The Weisses would not have to move after all. Grampa Drexel's life had been saved. And yet Mrs. Zimmermann and Rose Rita received no signal that they could return to their own time. "There must still be unfinished business," Mrs. Zimmermann said. "One other deed that Granny Wetherbee's ghost wanted us to perform. But what it is I couldn't say."

The two of them were sitting at the kitchen table, drinking steaming-hot tea. Rose Rita looked haggard and worn. "I know Mom's going to kill me when I get home," she said. "I've been gone for months! She'll never trust me to visit you again." She reached into her jeans pocket and took out a crumpled piece of paper. "As for unfinished business, do you think it might be this stupid treasure?"

Mrs. Zimmermann picked up the paper and unfolded it. Rose Rita had told her all about the *fraktur* writing, and she had looked at the original, but she could not figure out the meaning. "It could be," she said. She wrinkled her face. "It isn't a very good poem, is it?"

"It stinks," Rose Rita said. "I mean, look at how he spells 'live.' It looks like the Roman numeral fifty-four. He—" She broke off and grabbed the paper. "My gosh! That's it!" She dashed away from the table and ran through the house, screaming for Heinrich and Hilda.

The two of them came, together with Mr. and Mrs. Weiss and Grampa Drexel. "What is it?" Mrs. Weiss asked. "Such screaming and yelling and laughing you make, you would think that a young man had asked your papa for your hand—"

Rose Rita thumped the copy of the poem down on the table. "I solved the puzzle!" she said. "Look, it isn't a code at all—it's just in the way you read the poem! Read the first word of each line, going top to bottom! The *first* shall find riches!" She had a pencil stub in her jeans pocket. She pulled it out and underlined the first word of each line, like this:

To the Sons of Liberty, That They Mite
Discover the Welth of Freedom

Step ye sons of freedom smart;
Liv with liberty in your hart.
Paces the foe with heavy tred;
North, your countrymen are lying dead.
From Boston, from Concord, from Lexington,
Cottage and mansion send forth their sons.
Rock-hard the hart of the British soldier,
Then harder still are we, and bolder.
Line your rebelion with corage brave;
Great harts will live where our flag shall wave.
Tree and river shall hide our arms
And as ye hear war's loud alarms,
Mountain and hill, and valley so deep,
Dig like the foxx your den to keep.

For if we keep fayth, our people true,
Treasure of liberty must be our due.
This-Vers-Made-By-Heinrich-Weiss-MDCCLXXVIII
The-First-Shall-Find-Riches.

Hermann Weiss blinked and slowly read aloud, "Step fifty-four paces north from Cottage Rock, then line great tree and mountain. Dig for treasure. Well, what do you know!"

"Papa," said Mrs. Weiss, "the great tree must be the old oak that your mother would never let you and your brothers cut down!"

"I'll get the shovels," Mr. Weiss said.

The directions were still not terribly clear, but after a day of digging, Hermann Weiss shouted in excitement. From the hole they had dug, he and his sons hauled up a wooden chest, bound with brass that had long since turned green with age. They pried off the rusted lock. When they opened the chest, hundreds of golden coins gleamed up at them.

"Now," said a happy, panting Heinrich, "we are too rich to have to move, forever!"

Rose Rita and Mrs. Zimmermann had stood watching the proceedings. They followed the treasure hunters back to the house, the men staggering under the tremendous weight of the golden trove. The whole family crowded around the kitchen table, where Mr. Weiss excitedly began to count and stack the coins.

But Mrs. Zimmermann and Rose Rita lingered in the doorway, feeling wistful and sad. "Come," a kindly voice whispered. "I have something to show you."

It was Grampa Drexel, looking spry again. He led them upstairs to his room. He closed the door and had them sit down. "As you know, the neighbors destroyed all the magical items they found at Stoltzfuss's place," Grampa Drexel said. "All but the wax dolls and this." He reached into a drawer and pulled out a small round mirror. He handed it to Mrs. Zimmermann. "I have removed the evil spell that was cast over it. It is a good mirror now. And I think a friend of yours has something to say to you. I will wait outside." He rose and shuffled out.

Rose Rita stood up and looked over Mrs. Zimmermann's shoulder. The round mirror, much smaller than the square one, had a rosy glow in its depths. Slowly the glow intensified, and then suddenly a beautiful old woman's face looked out. Her hair was snowy white, and deep lines etched her face, but the black eyes were bright and lively. Rose Rita felt rather than heard the words the woman in the mirror spoke: "Thank you, my Florrie. You have righted the great wrong. Now you may return to your own time, and you may find what you wanted. For the last time, dear Florrie, good-bye."

"Wait!" Mrs. Zimmermann said. But the mirror went

dark, and a moment later it popped. A zigzag line now ran across it. Mrs. Zimmermann sighed. " 'The mirror crack'd from side to side,' " she said. Then she stood up briskly. "Bessie is waiting for us," she told Rose Rita. "And there's no time to lose!"

They did not pause to say good-bye to the excited Weiss family. Only Grampa Drexel saw them off. Rose Rita felt a little tearful. "I wanted to tell Hilda how much I liked her," she said. "And I never really thanked Heinrich. If he hadn't been such a good shot when he threw that sword, I wouldn't even be here!"

"They know how you feel," Grampa Drexel said kindly. "Now you must hurry. These things don't happen every day, you know. So go back to your home, and remember—you must believe hard, with all your heart, to get there!" He waved a farewell to them.

The weather had become springlike, and the long walk to Fuller's Hill was a warm one. They toiled up the road until they found the right clump of rhododendron, and then they climbed into Bessie. "I doubt if she'll even start after all this time," Mrs. Zimmermann grumbled. The car was a mess outside, with dirt and leaves and bird droppings all over it. It smelled lonely and cold inside, because the thick bushes had kept the warming sun off it. "Well," said Mrs. Zimmermann, "here goes nothing."

The engine started on the first try. Mrs. Zimmermann

revved it, and the radio crackled with static. Mrs. Zimmermann smiled. "One down. Now to get out of here."

She carefully backed the Plymouth out and, after a few minutes of maneuvering, turned it around. They crept back up the track. Soon they saw where the old mountain road curved hard to the left, away from the granite cliff. "What did Mr. Drexel say?" Mrs. Zimmermann asked. "Believe with all your heart? Well, right *there* is where the tunnel would be, if there were a tunnel, and so I believe that we'll head right for that cliff. Are you with me?"

Rose Rita swallowed. "Sure," she said.

"Here we go!" Mrs. Zimmermann wasn't kidding. She stomped on the accelerator, and Bessie leaped forward. The cliff seemed to roar toward them, faster and faster. Rose Rita grabbed the armrest and held it tight. *I believe, I believe,* she told herself. She wanted to close her eyes, but if she did—

The rock wall was just ahead of them!

Zoom! The car made that funny sound that cars make when they plunge into tunnels, and for an instant everything went dark. Then fluorescent lights flashed above the car, and a semicircle of hot summer daylight glared ahead of them. In a moment they burst out into the open air. On the radio an excited announcer bellowed, "Clyde Vollmer blasts it over the fence! What a game! A grand-slam home run for Vollmer, and the Red Sox take it eight to four after sixteen innings!"

"We're back!" Rose Rita screeched. "We're really and truly back!"

Mrs. Zimmermann pulled Bessie off onto the shoulder. Her hands were shaking. "We are," she said. "And that's the same baseball game we were listening to, weeks and weeks ago! Not a day has passed in 1951! Oh, thank you, Granny Wetherbee!"

The two of them had some planning to do. Rose Rita wanted to go straight to New Zebedee. She felt as if they had been away from home for weeks. However, Mrs. Zimmermann pointed out that as far as the world knew, they had not missed a day. In the end Rose Rita reluctantly agreed that they should go ahead with their tour, just as if nothing had happened.

So they turned around, and after a moment's hesitation they went through the tunnel again. This time they came out still on a modern highway. They found the site of the Weiss farm, because Cottage Rock still loomed there off to the left of the highway, but now the farm was a small village named Weissburg. They drove in and found it a charming little place. They ate at Harry and Betty Weiss's Cafeteria, and Mrs. Zimmermann talked to the owners. Harry Weiss was clearly a relative of Hermann's: He had the same broad red face and blue eyes. Harry told them that his family had lived here for ages, and he told them where the family cemetery was, not far outside of town. After some searching Mrs. Zimmermann and Rose Rita found the old graveyard, and after rambling through it they paused before a grave with an elegant marble headstone that read, "Wilhelm Peter Drexel, 1751–1844. Beloved stepfather."

Rose Rita felt very sad, but Mrs. Zimmermann said, "He lived his full span. He wasn't cut off in 1828. We actually changed history, and it wasn't all a dream or a hallucination."

But she must have felt sad too, because they didn't look for any other graves. The two of them continued their Penn Dutch vacation. They spent a couple of days in Stonebridge, where in a junk shop Mrs. Zimmermann found a broken old lamp with a base supported by three bronze claws. "Griffins' talons," she said. "Griffins' talons, or I don't know my talismans. Well, it won't give light, but griffins can be lucky animals to have around, so I'll pay a quarter for it."

The two of them enjoyed their vacation. The dark clouds of fear and despair had cleared. But a little sorrow still lingered in Rose Rita's heart. On their last night in Pennsylvania, in another tourist cabin, Mrs. Zimmermann suggested a game of chess. Rose Rita just shook her head and sighed.

"All right, young lady, that is *it!*" Mrs. Zimmermann said. "You are just about as much fun as a toothache. Rose Rita, what in heaven's name is the matter with you?"

With a miserable expression on her face Rose Rita said, "It's just that I messed everything up! I was gonna be so smart. I snooped around and got hexed by old Stoltzfuss. Then I fooled with magic and nearly got eaten by a demon. Then I did it again and nearly got Heinrich and myself killed. I shouldn't be trusted to do anything alone. I guess I need a keeper."

Mrs. Zimmermann snorted with irritation. "Nonsense. Now listen carefully, because I will say this only once. Everything you did, you did because you were trying to help Grampa Drexel, or the Weisses, or me. So what if it didn't work out as you planned? You *tried*—that's the important thing! And when everything went wrong, you coped with your troubles."

Rose Rita blinked. "But I should have asked for your advice and help—"

Mrs. Zimmermann held up a hand for silence. "Rose Rita, I will not always be around to help and advise you. A time comes when everyone must act all alone. That time came for you on this trip—and you were unselfish, and determined, and brave."

Rose Rita blinked. "Do you mean I'm on my own from now on?"

Mrs. Zimmermann threw her head back and laughed. "Of course not, you silly-billy. What did you tell me so long ago? 'I'm your friend, through thick and thin.' "

With a sniffle and a smile Rose Rita completed their rhyme: "To the bitter end! We'll see the bad times out and the good times in."

"That's right," Mrs. Zimmermann said, smiling.

"Well, the same goes here!" She put her hand out. "Shake on that!"

Rose Rita took her friend's hand, and from then on everything was all right again. The next day they drove back through Stonebridge and up Fuller's Hill. Just before they got to the tunnel that had once disappeared on them, Rose Rita had Mrs. Zimmermann pull off the road. "I don't know why you want to stop here," complained Mrs. Zimmermann. "I mean, I don't think we're going to go in this side and come out on the other in 2051 or anything."

Rose Rita climbed out of the car. Traffic was very light on this hot August day. The cliff side was familiar, and yet it was different too, because the last time she had been here had been on a moonlit night in late winter. But finally she found what she was searching for: very faint and ancient scratches showed on the rock face, long straight horizontal lines and vertical ones. They made a big + on the rock, and at the center of the plus sign was a small green cushion of moss.

"Get me something to dig with," said Rose Rita.

They made do with a screwdriver. What Rose Rita had hidden was still there, after all those years, at the bottom of a little pocket of earth packed into a natural hole in the rock. Rose Rita stood back. "Grampa Drexel said that you would have to be the first one to touch it. Reach in and get it."

With a questioning look Mrs. Zimmermann carefully

put her hand down into the hole. She pulled out something about the size of a golf ball. After she used a tissue to clean off the dirt, she found herself holding a crystal orb. "Rose Rita, what is this?" she asked in a tremulous voice.

"Something that Grampa Drexel made just for you."

Mrs. Zimmermann stood speechless with the crystal cupped in her hands. It flickered with a beautiful deep purple that shone clear and bright even in the summer sun. "Why, Rose Rita," she murmured. "I—I don't know how to thank—"

And then Mrs. Zimmermann and Rose Rita were hugging each other tight and laughing like maniacs. One or two cars went by, but none of them stopped. It was just as well. This was a very private moment of happiness, meant to be shared just by the two friends.

CHAPTER THIRTEEN

On a Monday morning two weeks after their return from Pennsylvania, Mrs. Zimmermann and Rose Rita were at the bus stop in front of Heemsoth's Rexall Drug Store to meet Jonathan and Lewis Barnavelt. The two had flown from London to New York, had taken the train to Toledo, and then had transferred to a Greyhound bus for the trip to New Zebedee, which was off the passenger-train route.

Rose Rita grinned as Lewis stepped down to the sidewalk. He looked grumpy, sweaty, and tired—just the way you should look when coming back from a long trip. But he caught sight of her and returned her grin. Behind him was a mussed-up Jonathan Barnavelt, his blue work shirt and his khaki wash pants wrinkled. His bushy red beard was crumpled on one side, where he had been leaning against the bus seat and sleeping. "Hello, Pruny!" he boomed as he lugged two huge suitcases off the bus. "And you too, Rose Rita. How's the gimpy leg?"

"It's all better," Rose Rita returned. "Good enough for me to beat Lewis in a race!"

Lewis gave her a friendly sort of dirty look. "We'll see about that."

They all climbed into Bessie, and Mrs. Zimmermann started the engine. "Hey," Uncle Jonathan objected when she turned left at the stoplight on Main Street. "This isn't the way home!"

"No," Mrs. Zimmermann said in a tart voice. Bessie clattered over the railroad tracks, and they were on the Homer Road. "It's the way out to my cottage at Lyon Lake. You boys could use a bath, a swim, and a good home-cooked meal before going back to Castle Barnavelt. Don't worry—Rose Rita and I gave the place a good going-over on Saturday, so everything is clean and ready for you. We even put Cheerios in the cupboard and milk in the refrigerator, so you'll be all set to 'cook' your own breakfasts!"

"Well," Jonathan said, "a bath and a swim do sound good at that. And we've got quite a story to tell you about our travels."

But during the drive out he would not say a word

about their trip, and neither would Lewis. Rose Rita kept glancing over at Lewis, who sat beside her in the backseat. He was subdued, and he stared out the window as the car rolled along. Something about him had changed. Rose Rita thought and thought, and then she noticed how his belt had a flappy tongue hanging out of the buckle. "You've lost weight!" she said.

Lewis started, then grinned sheepishly. "We walked a lot," he said. "All over the place. And most of the food . . ." He wrinkled his nose. "Did you know that in France they eat *snails*?" With a sigh he added, "It'll be great to have some normal food again."

Lewis had lost a good many pounds during his six weeks in Europe. He still wasn't exactly thin, but now he was more solid and chunky than fat. And Rose Rita thought he might have grown a little taller too.

As they parked in front of Mrs. Zimmermann's cottage and got out of the car, Jonathan said, "Florence, I have a confession to make. While we were in Germany, I managed to take a side trip to the University of Göttingen, where you took your degree. Do you remember Professor Athanasius there?"

Mrs. Zimmermann laughed. "Of course! 'Very goot, class. Und today ve begin a consideration uff alchemical thaumaturgy.' Good heavens, is he still there? He must be about a hundred years old!"

"Yes, he's still there, and no, he is not a hundred

years old. He's only eighty-two," Jonathan said as he helped Mrs. Zimmermann remove a heavy picnic hamper from the car trunk. He sighed. "I thought perhaps he might have some way of restoring your magic—no, don't object, I know it bothers you—but he couldn't think of a thing that wouldn't take seven or eight years to accomplish. Sorry."

Mrs. Zimmermann's eyes twinkled. "Well, we'll just have to live with it, Weird Beard. Don't let it bother you."

Lewis and Uncle Jonathan took turns bathing, and then everyone went for a swim in the lake. Lewis's dog-paddle style had not improved very much, but he perked up and enjoyed himself. He and Rose Rita raced, and he didn't seem to mind losing. Afterward Mrs. Zimmermann cooked hamburgers on a grill, and they all sat on the lawn and had a picnic lunch. Lewis ate three hamburgers and cast a wistful eye at a fourth, but he turned it down.

"Tell us about your trip," Rose Rita said. "Was it wonderful?"

Jonathan, full of hamburgers, leaned back and said, "Well, parts of it were. But I have a better idea. I won't just tell you about the sights—I'll show them to you." It took a little preparation, but soon they were all laughing at a sort of home-movie show. Except that the movies were Uncle Jonathan's magical illusions, three dimensional and so real it seemed as if you could touch them. The four friends saw the Changing of the Guard at Buckingham Palace (Uncle Jonathan mischievously gave one of the guards Lewis's face), and then a can-can dance from Paris (Rose Rita squealed to see that she and Mrs. Zimmermann were the last two high-kicking dancers on the right side), and then fairyland castles from Austria, the canals of Venice, and lots more.

"Not bad, Fuzzy Face," Mrs. Zimmermann said when the show had finished. She flicked a match from the air and lit one of her thin cigars. "At least *you* haven't lost your touch."

"Thanks, Haggy," Uncle Jonathan returned.

Rose Rita was curious about something. "You said only parts of the trip were wonderful. What happened that made the rest not so wonderful?"

Jonathan made a face. "Not now. Maybe Lewis and I will tell you that story some other day. But it's enough for me that we've been on a great, long journey, and we got homesick, and here we are again, with the two people we like most in the world—right, Lewis?"

Lewis blushed. "Yeah," he muttered gruffly, but he looked pleased.

Later Lewis and Rose Rita went for a walk along the edge of the lake. Rose Rita picked up a rock and skimmed it across the water, getting four good hops. Lewis tried, but his stone plunked down on the first splash.

"You have to throw with your arm level," Rose Rita said. "Sidearm, like this."

Lewis tried again, and finally he managed a couple of skips. "Thanks," he said.

"That's okay." After a moment Rose Rita added, "You know, I could teach you other stuff too. Like, well, how to dance, for instance."

Lewis looked away. Then he gave her an embarrassed glance. "Yeah, I guess that would be okay."

They walked back to the cottage, where Uncle Jonathan and Mrs. Zimmermann had just finished repacking Bessie. The green car gleamed in the afternoon sunlight. "Oh," Mrs. Zimmermann said. "I forgot one thing. Rose Rita, would you get it for me, please?"

"Sure," Rose Rita said, grinning. She and Mrs. Zimmermann had worked out this little surprise ahead of time. She took the keys from Mrs. Zimmermann, unlocked the front door, ran into the cottage, and came back with a folded black umbrella. "Here you are," she said, handing it over.

Uncle Jonathan looked puzzled. "What's this, Hagface? Isn't that the umbrella I gave you a couple of Christmases ago? I thought it was useless."

"I've made some modifications," Mrs. Zimmermann said. "Watch." She turned the umbrella upside down, and Uncle Jonathan and Lewis could see that the handle had been replaced by a bronze talon gripping a small crystal orb. A bright-magenta spark lurked at the center of the crystal. Mrs. Zimmermann held the umbrella straight out from her.

They all gasped. The umbrella suddenly became a tall staff, with a blinding purple star at its tip. Mrs. Zimmermann stood wrapped in billowing purple robes that flickered with crimson flame. She raised the wand and touched the hood of Bessie with the crystal. A pool of brilliant purple formed on the car's hood, and it spread out like a ripple on a pond, the purple washing over the green. In an instant the car's color had changed completely. In another instant Mrs. Zimmermann stood there with a broad smile on her face. She was wearing her normal purple floral-print summer dress again, and in her hand she held just a plain black umbrella.

Jonathan gave her a suspicious glance, then bent forward. "This isn't an illusion," he muttered. "It's a transformation! You've actually changed the paint! But when we left, you didn't have the power to change cream into butter!"

Rose Rita laughed. "Maybe we had our own adventures while you and Lewis were off in Europe."

Lewis was blinking like crazy. "Wow" was all he could say for the moment.

Uncle Jonathan ran his hand over the new paint job. "Dry as a bone, and it looks like five coats and a couple of good hard wax jobs!" Straightening, he said, "I see you two have a story to tell. All right, Prunella, give!"

"All in good time," Mrs. Zimmermann said in a happy voice. "Into the car now, and on the way back you'll hear the tale."

And so the four friends piled into the transformed automobile, and as Mrs. Zimmermann started the car and headed back to New Zebedee, she began to tell the story of the ghost in the mirror.

JOHN BELLAIRS

is the critically acclaimed, best-selling author of many Gothic novels, *The Curse of the Blue Figurine; The Mummy, the Will, and the Crypt; The Lamp from the Warlock's Tomb; The Spell of the Sorcerer's Skull; The Revenge of the Wizard's Ghost; The Chessmen of Doom; The Eyes of the Killer Robot;* and the previous novels starring Lewis Barnavelt, Rose Rita Pottinger, and Mrs. Zimmermann: *The House with a Clock in Its Walls; The Figure in the Shadows;* and *The Letter, the Witch, and the Ring.*

John Bellairs died in 1991. However there are several more books that Mr. Bellairs left that Dial will be publishing. Brad Strickland, a longtime Bellairs fan, will be completing them, just as he did *The Ghost in the Mirror.*